"Why haven't **ever married, Lawton?**

"I've never met anyone for whom I'd exchange my freedom." He shrugged, his eyes wary.

He can't believe *I'm* trying to trap him, she thought bitterly. "I won't ever marry," she muttered aloud, hoping to convince him.

"Neale!" he retorted. "You can't go on believing your ex-fiancé has ruined your life." His arms went suddenly around her. "It's not something you can bottle up forever. Tell me about it."

His arms were persuasive, and she'd never expected to have them around her again. With a sob she relaxed against him as his kindness proved too much for her. She began telling him little things, then couldn't seem to stop.

She could actually feel the deep ice that had been so long inside her, permanently dissolving....

Books by Margaret Pargeter

These books may be available at your local bookseller.

Don't miss any of our special offers. Write to us at the following address for information on our newest releases.

Harlequin Reader Service
P.O. Box 52040, Phoenix, AZ 85072-2040
Canadian address: P.O. Box 2800, Postal Station A,
5170 Yonge St., Willowdale, Ont. M2N 6J3

MARGARET PARGETER

total surrender

Harlequin Books

TORONTO • NEW YORK • LONDON
AMSTERDAM • PARIS • SYDNEY • HAMBURG
STOCKHOLM • ATHENS • TOKYO • MILAN

Harlequin Presents first edition May 1985
ISBN 0-373-10788-9

Original hardcover edition published in 1984
by Mills & Boon Limited

CHAPTER ONE

'YOU'RE sure we've got everything, Neale?' Rex Fuller fussed as they sped to the boardroom.

'I think so,' Neale Curtis replied breathlessly, grimacing wryly at the bulging portfolio of colour schemes she was carrying and managing to hide her irritation that a mere summons to Lawton Baillie's presence was enough to send Rex into near panic. 'If we have forgotten anything,' she reassured him, 'I'll come back for it. It's not as though we're going to be miles away.'

Rex glanced at her impatiently. 'Do you really imagine Mr Baillie's going to sit cooling his heels while you fetch something we should have had with us in the first place?'

Neale sighed, 'He can't eat you.'

'Nothing so humane,' Rex retorted tersely, 'Slow torture's more in his line.'

Neale was silent as they stepped into the lift which would take them to the top floor. She refused to encourage Rex's foolish apprehension though she had to admit she had never met Mr Baillie. Her previous position in the firm had scarcely been important enough to warrant such an honour. It was only by dint of sheer hard work combined with the coincidence of other personnel leaving that she had been promoted to being Rex Fuller's right-hand assistant in the design department. From now on, she realised, meetings with the heads of the other departments might become a regular occurrence.

It wasn't often though that the hierarchy included the highest of them all, the thirty-eight year old chairman and owner of the firm, the well-known tycoon, Lawton

Baillie. Hotels were his main thing, he collected them as other men might collect stamps. He bought old, obsolete ones which he renovated and developed, as well as building from scratch on some of the world's most beautiful sites. To achieve this he ran his own construction company along with a team of architects and interior designers, of whom Neale was one.

It was October and in a few months a huge hotel on the coast would be nearing completion and, according to Rex, Mr Baillie was taking a greater than usual interest in it. This must be why Rex was acting like a slave-driver, working his department flat out. For weeks now he had never let up and Neale for one was feeling the strain.

Several of the directors were already in the boardroom when Rex and Neale arrived but, as yet, there was no sign of Lawton Baillie. Breathing a sigh of relief, Neale slid unobtrusively into a chair just as he entered. Fascinated, her eyes widened as they clung to him. The men round her automatically rose to their feet but for some inexplicable reason Neale's legs were suddenly too weak to allow her to join them. She could only hope that Mr Baillie would think she was taking advantage of the fact that she was a female.

A peculiar shiver ran through her as she briefly studied his tallness and darkness before lowering her eyes. The occasional, rather bad photographs she had seen of him had given no indication of how his actual physical presence would affect her. She would never have believed such raw sexuality could emanate from a man if she hadn't experienced it herself. Lawton Baillie might be dressed formally in a tailored grey suit but it did nothing to hide his overpowering masculinity.

There was a general scraping of chairs as everyone sat down again but, despite the relaxed atmosphere produced by a light remark from him, Neale had to take a deep breath before she could bring herself to look again in his direction.

To her dismay he was staring at her, brows faintly drawn over deep-set, dark blue eyes. He was good-looking but the planes of his face might have been chiselled from iron, so tightly was the skin stretched over commanding cheekbones and a square, aggressive chin. His mouth was thin but somehow supported the impression of sensuousness given out by the taut proportions of his magnificent body.

Neale swallowed, unconsciously lifting a hand to the heavy coil of hair at her nape, making sure it was tidy. Lawton Baillie was making her aware of herself as no other man had managed to do in a long time. Startled to realise this, she quickly withdrew her hand, wondering what on earth had got into her?

Returning his curious stare with as much coolness as she could muster, she forced herself to endure the slow thoroughness of his exploratory glance. For what seemed like hours but could only have been seconds, he studied her youthful slenderness before turning to Rex.

'Is this your new assistant?'

'Yes,' Rex introduced them eagerly, 'Miss Curtis took over when Mrs Talbot left. But I believe I told you . . .?'

'Did you deliberately mislead me?' Lawton Baillie enquired impassively, 'I distinctly recall you referring to your new assistant as Neale Curtis.'

'Neale happens to be a girl's name as well as a man's,' Neale explained hastily, then flushed as a dark brow lifted sardonically, wishing she had kept quiet.

'Ah, it's one of those, is it? I expect it's spelt differently?' Lawton Baillie smiled at her while the members of his staff glanced at her with increasing interest.

'Yes,' she mumbled, ready to sink through the floor.

'How differently?' he drawled, enjoying her discomfort, she could see.

Huskily she spelt out her name, apprehensive of what was to follow, but to her surprise he merely nodded, as if losing interest, and got on with the business.

The hotel under discussion was the one due for completion on the south coast. If it proved a success it would be enlarged, meanwhile the interior decor of over a hundred rooms and suites had to be approved and finalised. Soon the table was littered with colour schemes and plans, all of which Lawton Baillie appeared to consider. On the whole he seemed favourably impressed. It was only the decoration of some of the more expensive accommodation that he openly opposed.

'These suites,' he tapped Neale's drawings with long, steely fingers, 'I believe they were designed with honeymoon couples and people enjoying carefree holidays in mind. Would dark browns and blacks appeal to you on your honeymoon, Miss Curtis?'

Neale was furious that she should find herself flushing each time he spoke to her. She had thought the habit conquered long ago. She also wished he had kept the sarcasm she had sensed out of his voice when he asked such a question. Mostly she wished he hadn't addressed it to her at all. She and Rex had disagreed over the colour schemes for these particular suites but Rex had been adamant. If she told Mr Baillie this she would feel she was betraying Rex who, on the whole, was a very considerate man to work for.

'I haven't been on a honeymoon, Mr Baillie,' she murmured, hoping this would suffice.

It didn't. Immediately he came back. 'Do you mean you aren't married, or simply that you didn't have time to go away? Rex introduced you as Miss Curtis,' he met her puzzled gaze blandly, 'but women don't always use their married names in business.'

'I'm not married, Mr Baillie,' she had to clench her hands to stop from glaring at him mutinously. He must know perfectly well he was embarrassing her yet he seemed to be getting a kind of perverted pleasure out of it.

He viewed her pink cheeks derisively, showing no

remorse. Instead he persisted relentlessly. 'Well most young women dream of being married and having a glamorous honeymoon. So what makes you think that the average bride with her head in the clouds wishes to be plunged into a nightmare of drab colours? The unreal world newly-weds usually live in rarely lasts, but you seem determined not to give them a chance.'

Luckily Rex intervened—not before time! Neale thought. 'I'm afraid I'm to blame, Mr Baillie,' he stammered, 'I—I believed, mistakenly it seems, that because of the recession you'd prefer something practical.'

'That's just where you're wrong, Rex,' his boss replied coolly. 'If you paid more attention to our market research and the way my present policies pay off, you would realise if we stuck to being practical you might soon be out of a job. On holiday people wish to be cheered up, not constantly reminded, by the psychological effect of brown walls and black carpets, of the possibly dull existence they've managed to escape from for a couple of weeks.'

While Neale seethed, Rex nodded glumly but added with a hint of stubbornness. 'I still feel anything too opulent. . . .'

'Rex!' Lawton interrupted, his voice harder than it had been. 'For this type of accommodation people are going to be paying a packet. They will expect something opulent to justify their expenditure. I know when I pay over the odds for something,' his eyes lit for a moment on Neale, 'I hate to be disappointed.'

Neale didn't want to feel there was anything personal in the brief glance slanted at her but all the same she shivered. She was beginning to hate Lawton Baillie for being able to get a reaction from her merely by looking in her direction. She almost jumped when he spoke to her.

'Any further comment to make, Miss Curtis?'

She shook her head, refraining from pointing out

that those who could afford holidays in Baillie hotels couldn't possibly come from the kind of background he had implied.

If the scornful flash in her eyes betrayed her, apart from a faint tightening of his lips, Lawton Baillie gave no indication that he guessed what she was thinking. After another slight pause, during which he cruelly watched the colour come and go in her cheeks, he proposed they adjourn for lunch.

He kept them hard at it all afternoon. Neale, having been given to understand that he usually took little interest in the actual decor of his hotels, being content to leave it to the experts, was amazed at the depth to which he probed the completion of this one. By five she was exhausted and welcomed the intrusion of the tea trolley.

She carried her tea over to the window in order to stretch her legs and get rid of an unusual feeling of tension. She felt mangled though Rex had taken the brunt of the punishment. When he had muttered it could have been worse, she failed to believe him. It wasn't only the colour schemes for the suites that was wrong. In several other areas their work had been criticised.

'Problems, Miss Curtis?'

Neale nearly dropped her cup, she was so startled to find Lawton Baillie behind her. Turning too quickly, a flash of anger went through her, as again, like a physical thing, his eyes roamed her body. Being slim and delicately built, she didn't think there was enough of her to command such attention.

Pulling herself together, she tried to answer his query coolly. 'Not now, Mr Baillie. I can't think of a single problem you haven't dealt with very efficiently.'

He smiled at the acidity in her voice which she had tried unsuccessfully to hide but his glance remained keen. 'I could have sworn you were working something out?'

Close at hand he was even more intimidating than he had been across the boardroom and luncheon tables. She jerked a step back, feeling immediately threatened. The impression was so realistic that the hand holding her cup shook and a few drops of tea spilt annoyingly into her saucer.

'Nervous, Miss Curtis?' dark blue eyes rested speculatively on her trembling hands, 'I shouldn't have thought a little criticism would affect you so adversely?'

To deny it would be a waste of time. This man saw too much and too clearly. 'It's been a long day,' she hedged shortly.

His mouth quirked. 'Rex has just been telling me you never mind how long a day is.'

'There are days and days, Mr Baillie,' she replied dryly, regaining some outward composure while continuing to quake inwardly. Not since the morning of her nineteenth birthday, when Tony had failed to turn up at church for their wedding, had she felt so disturbed by a man. Since then she had managed to keep all men at a distance. She might work with them, she even socialised with them at the odd office party she couldn't get out of attending, but she never let any one of them get really near her. She believed she had grown a cast-iron immunity and couldn't understand how Lawton Baillie was making her pulse flutter.

'Did my insistence that the honeymoon suites be decorated differently really bother you?' he asked blandly.

She flushed, conscious of his eyes studying the smooth perfection of her skin. Defensively she retorted, 'I think Rex was aiming for sophistication rather than——,' she remembered the word he'd used, 'drabness. Perhaps if we'd been aware you had some specific purpose in mind. . . .'

He ignored this and laughed. 'I thought you would have used your imagination?'

She stiffened. 'I don't have that kind of imagination, Mr Baillie.'

'No?' again the hateful tilt of a doubtful brow, 'Maybe you and I should spend a honeymoon somewhere? There's nothing like a taste of the real thing for stimulating jaded inspiration.'

Neale suspected he was goading her deliberately but this didn't stop her from exclaiming angrily. 'I can do without that kind of stimulation, thank you!'

'Ah,' a faint gleam in his eye hinted infuriatingly that he was enjoying her temper, 'A frigid young lady?'

'I was once engaged. . . .'

'So . . .' he said softly, 'I mightn't have been serious about our going away together but why the outrage?'

Neale was aghast. It had been years since she had allowed herself even to think of her ill-fated engagement yet here she was mentioning it to a relative stranger! And of course he believed, as many people did, that engaged couples frequently slept together. Well, let him think what he liked! He would probably disparage her more if he learned the truth!

'You're my boss, Mr Baillie,' she said almost defiantly, 'but that doesn't give you the right to poke fun at me!'

He looked at her taut face with enigmatic eyes. 'I don't think I want to poke fun at you, Neale. Why not dine with me this evening and we can begin again?'

Incredulously Neale stared at him. 'Why?'

'Haven't I just said?'

Unconvinced, she shook her head. 'Saying sorry is one thing but you don't have to go to such lengths.'

The hard, sensuous lips twisted slightly. 'There must be a mirror somewhere round or perhaps you would like me to spell it out? You're a beautiful girl, Neale, and I want to know you better.'

'Even if this were true,' Neale's remarkable grey eyes were full of doubt, 'you surely don't ask every attractive woman you meet to go out with you?'

'Some I do,' he answered casually, 'But most of them don't interest me much.'

He couldn't be asking her to believe that! 'I'm sure we don't have much in common either,' she said soberly, appearing to take him at his word. She was actually thinking that in her case, she would never have the sophistication or intelligence to keep him interested for even a few minutes.

'We'll never know unless we make an attempt to find out,' he countered coolly. 'I'll pick you up at eight.'

'No thank you, Mr Baillie,' suddenly overcome by a surge of panic that ignored common sense, Neale fled. Grabbing her already packed portfolio, she avoided Rex's questioning glance and with a vague goodnight aimed at the rest of the company, hastily left the room.

Tuesday and Wednesday proved hectic. Neale occasionally wondered if she would ever survive. In the design department they followed a tight schedule all the time. Having to change anything made a lot of extra work but altering the decor of hotel suites was quite a big job. She knew Rex was worried about it though he didn't say much. When he answered the phone on Thursday and she saw the frown on his face, she wondered anxiously if it was more bad news?

Replacing the receiver, Rex groaned. 'I don't know how much more I can take.'

'What is it?' she asked apprehensively.

'Baillie!' he replied briefly, helplessly throwing up his hands, 'He wants me to go to the Med. and you to have lunch with him.'

She didn't know which sounded the worst. 'Why?' she faltered numbly. Surely Rex couldn't be away, not with so many important decisions to be made here? And as for lunching with Lawton Baillie, well, she didn't want to even think about it!

'It's the Miranda, in Spain,' Rex shrugged. 'Apparently he's been building some self-catering units instead of expanding the actual hotel. He wants me to go and have a look at them so I'll be able to begin on them as soon as this south coast job's finished.'

'But why the rush?' Neale gazed at him in bewilderment, 'And don't you think it strange that Mr Baillie should speak to you himself? I mean he doesn't usually bother with such things.'

'Oh, occasionally he does,' Rex murmured vaguely, his mind obviously already halfway to Spain. 'He's like that, you never know what he's up to.'

'After the fiasco he considers we made of these suites,' bitterly she tapped the scaled-down plans on a design board, 'he must believe we're desperately in need of his personal supervision!'

'Oh, come!' Rex laughed, eyeing Neale's indignant face tolerantly, 'He's not as bad as all that. But that's why he wants you to have lunch with him. He wants to hear what progress we're making. One-thirty at the Grosvenor, in Park Lane, so don't grumble! It could have been worse.'

Could it? Neale wondered unhappily, making her way there at the appropriate hour. She supposed she could be thankful she had settled that morning on her one reasonably smart suit when it might easily have been the jeans and cotton smocks she frequently wore. She assured herself that this was because Lawton Baillie would expect her to be stylishly dressed, not because she had any particular desire to look nice for him.

Rex had already left for Spain, confessing he might have enjoyed the break if he hadn't promised to take Meg out that evening. Meg was his wife and they adored each other but she hated it when his work took him out of the country.

To Neale's surprise, when she reached the Grosvenor, Lawton was there before her. When she was shown into the bar, he was lounging against it, his eyes on the door. As she paused in the doorway, he looked at her for a moment then straightened and smiled. With his glance raking over her, her breath caught, exactly as it had done the first time she had seen him.

He left his drink to come to her and her pulse raced as her eyes locked with his. She felt dazed as he walked easily towards her, like a panther with his lean, muscular frame. She stood stock-still as shock of a kind she hadn't met before washed over her, making her dizzy. He was just as handsome as she remembered, his eyes as incredibly blue, his face just as hard.

Her suit was severely tailored but the fine silky blouse she wore with it she had bought in a moment of weakness. It betrayed her constant fight against being too feminine but sometimes she couldn't resist wearing it. She wished she didn't have it on today, as Lawton Baillie's eyes explored its low neckline. At the taunting appreciation in his eyes, her cheeks warmed to a matching soft pink. She could feel unwanted waves of heat consuming her and recoiled sharply. Numbly she stared at him, thinking apprehensively, that she must be going down with something.

He didn't let her recoil far. He must have been aware of her inclination to run for his hand went straight for her arm. 'I'm glad you managed to make it,' he said smoothly.

'Rex relayed your message,' she replied stiffly. 'It didn't seem to leave me much choice.'

The strong mouth quirked in amusement. 'If I hadn't made it an order, would you have come? I seem to recall you aren't fond of accepting my invitations?'

There had only been one! 'I have to eat,' she murmured woodenly.

'My thoughts exactly,' he drew her mockingly closer. 'You look charming,' again his glance lingered on the smooth column of her throat, 'I like your pearls.'

'A legacy,' she managed to find her voice, 'My grandmother left them to me.'

'Very nice,' he guided her to a table near the bar but didn't let go of her until she was seated. 'What are you drinking?' he asked.

Thick dark lashes flickered uncertainly under feathery

winged brows of the same shade, 'I'll have anything. I don't mind.'

He ordered two Martinis with a teasing glint in his eyes. 'Somehow I got the impression you were a young lady with a mind of her own?'

She shrugged without answering, not sure if this was true anymore. 'I don't drink much so I'm no expert.'

'Only at deviation,' he laughed and, as their drinks arrived,.changed the subject. 'Do you always wear your hair like that?'

'Not always,' she replied, 'but I have to for work. There's such a lot of it.'

He studied the thick gleaming strands closely. 'Dare I ask when you allow it its freedom?'

Neale's cheeks went hot again, knowing he had guessed it was usually only in bed. The conversation had a degree of intimacy she found disturbing. And, although he didn't touch her, his eyes rested on her sensitive mouth, making her tremble. Something in his expression was melting her bones. In moments he had her wishing she could be in his arms, receiving his kisses on the soft fullness of her lips. As his glance grew more intent, as if he might actually be sharing her unconscious yearning, she reminded herself sharply she was twenty-three, no longer an impressionable school-girl. Tony had left her on the altar. Never would she forget the pitying glances of the wedding guests, the terrifying panic she had experienced to be followed afterwards by a bitterness such as she had never known existed. Her pride had been trampled in the dust and the sympathy she had received had somehow only made it worse. She had vowed, on sobbing knees, never to let a man near her again and until now she had kept that vow.

With a bright smile she ignored Lawton's query and reached for her drink. 'We've all been working hard on the new colour schemes. I'm sure you'll be happy with what we've achieved, so far.'

Dark brows rose but otherwise he gave no indication of being aware that she was attempting to steer the conversation to less intimate channels. For a while they talked business, until a waiter came to inform them their table was ready.

If she had hoped he would stick to the intricacies of interior decoration, she was doomed to disappointment. As soon as they began eating he commented thoughtfully. 'You told me you were once engaged. What happened?'

Who else would have the nerve to ask! Or the nerve to sound really interested. She wished she could avoid the astuteness of his eyes. She felt like a mouse looking for a hole and none available.

'What usually happens?' she shrugged, 'We changed our minds . . .' at least Tony had, and he couldn't have done it nearer the last minute. He had preferred someone else but she couldn't bear to confess this to Lawton Baillie. No one in the office knew, she hadn't told anyone. This was why she had come to London, to get her degree and find complete anonymity. She wasn't going to give away her shameful secret now.

'Had you known each other a long time?' he pressed. 'You can't have been that old—unless it happened recently?'

'I was nineteen,' she replied tersely. Then, almost against her will, 'We'd known each other since we were children.'

'Maybe you knew each other too well,' he said gently, 'How long were you lovers?'

Neale's cheeks flushed wildly. 'We weren't,' she felt like shouting, only to find she couldn't. It would be even more humiliating to confess she was still a virgin.

'D-don't you consider anything sacred, Mr Baillie?' she retorted, trying to speak coolly and angrily regretful of her betraying stammer.

'Sometimes it helps to talk about something like this,' he smiled, 'Call me Lawton.'

There was such a world of compassion in his eyes, it made her feel ashamed of herself, until she realised it could be a trap. She inhaled sharply. 'My private life is no concern of yours, Mr Baillie. I work for you and appreciate the generous salary you pay me but I don't consider that entitles you to pry into my past.'

He rebuked her quietly. 'I can't believe that showing an interest in one of my employees could be called prying, Miss Curtis.' He went on so softly she was briefly disarmed, 'You present an enigma bound to arouse curiosity. Look at you,' his glance moved significantly over her, 'That suit is so severely tailored it almost completely denies your femininity. It's just your frilly blouse that gives you away. Obviously your broken engagement affected you deeply but isn't it better to recognise a mistake and come to terms with it?'

'A typically male point of view!' she retorted.

He studied her tense face. 'Is it all men you dislike, Neale, or only me?'

His cool tones brought her to her senses. Dismayed, she took a fortifying sip of wine. She had been rude to Lawton once too often and his tolerance might not be unending. He would be used to women responding to his undoubted charm, smiling at him instead of snapping, as she was doing. He was the boss, in a much stronger position than she was. She must learn to control the irrational panic which overtook her each time he asked a personal question, otherwise she might be in danger of losing her job.

'I'm sorry,' she said quickly, 'I didn't mean to snap. I apologise.'

He smiled, as if he knew she hadn't answered his last question, but to her relief he didn't ask it again. But just as she was hoping he might be content to return to business, he disconcerted her by stretching out a hand to raise her drooping chin. 'Haven't you ever met anyone else? The past isn't always easy to forget on one's own.'

'Perhaps I learned a lesson,' as he released her chin, the tingling impression of his fingers lingered and it wasn't easy to keep her voice steady.

'Once bitten, twice shy,' he mused. 'With your looks you should have had the confidence to try again,'

She flinched with pain and resentment. 'I decided to concentrate on my career.'

'You've certainly done well,' his eyes never left her face. 'You look about seventeen. I find it difficult to believe you're twenty-four and a dedicated career woman.'

Frowning, Neale asked, 'How do you know my age, Mr Baillie?'

'As your employer I have access to all relevant data.'

She nodded. 'I am twenty-four, in a few weeks time,' she spoke as though she hadn't thought of it before and the knowledge puzzled her.

'There, you see,' his smile was taunting. 'When a woman starts denying her age it's time she began doing something about it. Otherwise she wakes up one morning and discovers it's too late.'

Neale flushed and clenched her hands. What was it about this man that aroused her almost to violence? 'I've a long way to go before I catch up with you,' she snapped maliciously.

His grin widened. 'I'm thirty-eight, quite a way ahead of you, but the years don't matter so much with a man. It may be unfair but it's one of life's little facts that no woman has yet been able to change.'

She had known this, of course, and again chided her runaway tongue that had a depressing habit of working against her. As a waiter interrupted with their coffee, she studied Lawton Baillie's austere features without realising what she was doing. He might be thirty-eight but his looks were backed by a vibrant vitality she could almost feel. Sometimes his eyes seemed to glow like those of a jungle cat, while the hard planes of his face hid demonic shadows that made her shiver.

Dressed in a grey suit, as severely cut as her own, he carried a quiet air of authority, with more power and self-confidence than she had ever seen in anyone before. When his glance rose to meet hers and something quivered between them, she gulped nervously and tore her eyes away.

Pretending to be watching her coffee, she murmured, as though casually, 'We don't see much of you in London.'

'I'm around.'

Such enigmatic tones could only mean he knew what was going on and somehow she didn't doubt it! Licking dry lips, she persevered. If she didn't take the initiative, he might begin asking more questions she didn't wish to answer. 'You spend a lot of time abroad?'

'Where most of my business is,' he seemed more interested in the lips she had moistened.

She swallowed convulsively. 'Or to escape our murky fogs?'

He laughed, placing a hand gently over her slender, artistic fingers as they lay on the table. 'You shouldn't let the weather enter your very soul. There's more to life than ambition and work, you know.'

'But nothing as satisfying,' as she sought unsuccessfully to free her hand, her eyes dared him to deny it.

His brows rose derisively. 'Didn't your fiancé teach you anything?'

She flushed as his meaning seemed very clear and snatched her hand away, not caring if he was offended. Tony had tried to teach her a lot, even the night before their wedding which had never taken place, he had begged her to sleep with him. This was one of the things she had found most impossible to forgive, and why her hatred overflowed to other men. Tony had been in love with another girl but this hadn't stopped him from trying to seduce her, even when he must have known he was leaving her!

'You know I'd rather not talk about my past,' she said stubbornly.

'Very well,' watching her hot cheeks paling, he appeared to come to a decision. 'We can go back to business again, if it will make you happier. Tomorrow we're both going down to the new hotel. I want to make sure you get it right this time.'

It didn't make her any happier but, apart from protesting that Rex might have liked to have been there—a remark Lawton totally ignored—Neale had no other option but to go with him. After a busy morning, mostly spent trying to persuade the rest of the staff they could manage in her absence, she joined him, after lunch, in the staff car park.

The roads were quiet once they were clear of the city. Lawton handled the big car he drove expertly and they reached the coast very quickly. Neale had been here before, with Rex, but she felt like a VIP arriving with the chairman of the company. She noticed that Lawton was on very easy terms with the site manager and how many of the other men spoke to him deferentially. Rex had mentioned that Lawton frequently visited his new sites, which might explain why he was so well known.

'Don't you think you're being very ambitious?' she asked, slightly bemused as she followed him through the vast conglomeration of concrete and bricks. She saw swimming pools yet to be filled, a sports complex and grounds in the final stages of completion. She shuddered at the amount of money being invested without any guarantee that such a venture would succeed.

'Don't you have any faith in my judgment?' he teased, making her feel a fool. 'The whole of life is a gamble, Neale,' he glanced at her dryly, 'Only some of us play for high stakes. Actually the odds against a project like this succeeding can be worked out fairly accurately beforehand on computers, so the risk is negligible really.'

'You can't provide the glamour of being in a foreign country, though, can you?' Neale frowned.

'Not here, for the British,' he agreed. 'But aren't you forgetting we have a lot of overseas visitors for whom the UK is a foreign country? And they don't always wish to spend all their time in London.'

Entering the hotel, he steered her through armies of workmen to the first floor, where most of the suites were. She marvelled that Lawton never once took a wrong turning, but then he had that kind of brain! In one of the largest suites he prepared to leave her.

'Got everything?' he asked, watching her opening the light case she was carrying and taking out her sketch pads. She had brought a dozen, just to impress him but he sounded more amused than anything else.

'Yes,' she replied.

He continued looking at her for another long moment while she studiously avoided meeting his eyes. 'I occasionally allow one mistake but never two,' he said softly.

His voice was so gentle, she was bewildered by the fear it shot through her. Apprehensively she jerked upright to stare at him. 'I'll do my best,' she exclaimed, 'But aren't you being rather unfair?'

It never paid to challenge one's boss, not if one had any sense at all, that is! He smiled, and she was reminded of a tiger moving in for the kill. 'As it's the same rule which you apparently apply to yourself, Neale, can you question the fairness of it?'

CHAPTER TWO

IT amazed Neale that Lawton Baillie had made such a success of his life. It was rumoured that his staff—those who worked closely with him—idolised him, but Neale couldn't see it! Certainly he was no psychologist. Someone should tell him that if he was rich he might be even richer if he was nice to the lower ranks of his employees instead of making them angry every chance he got!

Some time passed before Neale was able to forget his parting remark and get down to what she was supposed to be doing. It wasn't easy, but then nothing about this project had been. 'You win some, you lose some,' she found herself muttering aloud, rejecting as many sheets as she filled. If they finished up with scarlet ceilings and graffiti on the walls, Lawton would only have himself to blame!

She concentrated until she was sure the light was beginning to fade along with the noise the workmen were making. Wandering to the window, she gazed longingly at the sea, a hundred yards away. The beach beckoned and she decided to go for a walk. It was such a beautiful autumnal day, it might have been summer.

She was standing looking at the waves when she heard footsteps behind her. The hair on the back of her head prickled in awareness and she turned sharply.

'Do you make a habit of creeping up on people?' she asked, meeting a pair of dark blue eyes resentfully.

Lawton laughed. 'I was walking, not creeping, and if you'd had any warning you might have disappeared.'

'Why should I?'

He laughed again at her indignant tones. 'One of the first things I learnt was how to approach people.'

'You mean stalk people!'

He grinned. 'Some are easier than others.'

It was a crazy conversation, so why did she have to prolong it? 'You move so silently.'

'Not a crime, is it?' he glanced thoughtfully down at his feet. 'Perhaps you can tell me how to make a noise walking over sand?'

She smiled wryly, thinking it was time she let the matter rest. Her eyes began wandering over him. The black trousers and shirt he was wearing made him look like a pirate. There was something strong and untamed about him. His shoulders were broad, his chest deep, his balance easy on long, muscular legs. If she hadn't known who he was, she might have associated him with the sea or the land, rather than the city.

Trying to steady her treacherous pulse, she hastily averted her wayward eyes. 'I suppose you've come to tell me I shouldn't be here?'

'It occurred to me,' his mouth twitched but he looked at her solemnly. 'You can't be setting a very good example.'

She thought he was angry with her again and said unhappily. 'The men were going home and I longed for a breath of fresh air. I don't think they noticed.'

'I'll forgive you,' he teased. 'This time.'

'I had finished all I was able to do,' she assured him earnestly. 'The light was going.'

He nodded. 'That's why I came to look for you. We may as well go home too.'

'Yes,' she gazed at the sea wistfully. 'It's so quiet here and restful. I wish I had a tent.'

He glanced at her curiously. They were some distance from the hotel and there was nothing but empty stretches of sand. A sea bird wheeled above their heads, it's cry lonely and haunting. 'You feel some affinity with that bird?'

She followed it's solitary flight. 'A little.'

'You shouldn't, at your age. It's unhealthy.'

Sharply her eyes returned to his face, resenting the implications of what he had said while pretending to misunderstand him. 'I wasn't seriously considering it but surely camping out can't be unhealthy?'

His mouth tightened briefly, as though he knew perfectly well she was aware that wasn't what he meant. 'Okay,' he smiled tauntingly, 'I can easily play it your way. Let's pretend we're going to spend a night on the beach—shipwrecked or by choice, I don't mind. You realise you'll have to change your image?'

'My—image?'

'Don't look so startled, Miss Curtis,' he laughed. 'You can't rough it in a tent looking like a prim and proper schoolmarm, if such creatures exist any more? You'll have to take the pins out of your hair, for a start.'

However had she come to be blessed with such a boss? She backed in alarm. 'No!'

Her hands came up to push him off but his were quicker. Catching them, he held her still, removing the offending pins himself. During the whole operation she stood like a mesmerised rabbit. As soon as he touched her, her heart began pounding and her breath shortened. She had thought he was crazy, now she wondered if she was?

The last pin was disposed of before she found her voice. 'What did you do that for? A joke's a joke but you go—too far!'

He watched the masses of hair tumbling over her shoulders, the last rays of the sun turning it to gold. 'I wanted to see it.'

His voice was husky and her eyes darkened. She tried to make a light remark on the absurdity of the situation but couldn't. Where this man was concerned, her defences were hopelessly inadequate. She hadn't realised how inadequate until now. She began making silent vows. Never would she put herself in such a vulnerable position again. Lawton Baillie was experienced. He was also, for some reason, bored and looking for entertainment. Well, he must go and find someone else. He wasn't amusing himself at her expense!

He was still holding her and she protested tersely. 'Do you mind!'

He ignored her plea to be released, his eyes still on her hair. 'It's beautiful. I wonder what it's like spread over a pillow?'

She jumped in real fright, her slight body trembling. 'That's one thing you'll never find out!'

He smiled, deepening her suspicion he was only in this for amusement. 'You can't keep on running away.'

'I'm not!'

'Don't shout. The seagulls don't like it. Have you any idea what you're running from?'

Grey eyes blazed. 'I'm not running from anything. I just don't like being touched!'

The teasing note dropped from his voice leaving it rough-edged with impatience. 'You can't know until you try.'

How dared he! 'I tried once!'

'Fine!' he snapped back, 'So you did, so you did! And it was a failure. And you got hurt. So what's the big deal about that? Plenty get badly hurt every day and still have the guts to try again.'

'Again?'

'And again!' he stared into her incredulous face. 'It's called living, Neale.'

'The way I don't want to.'

He positively jeered, his blue eyes scorching. 'Why not say what you're thinking, that the choice is yours? Of course it is. You just sit and watch the world go by, a modern Lady of Shallot, and one day you see someone you want and you've lost the ability to go after him, to communicate on a level that brings response from a man. Then you'll have to learn to live with regret for the rest of your life, which will be much harder to endure than hurt pride.'

It must be the lecture of the year. And for her ultimate good or he wouldn't have made it. But it hadn't done any good. If anything Neale felt more frozen than before. She gazed up at him, her eyes huge with shock, slowly glazing with tears.

'Do you hear me?' he asked.

'I hear you,' she replied numbly, 'but you don't make sense.'

His hands slid from her hair, one to circle her nape while the other moved over her face. He explored the fine bones, smoothed feathery brows, drew a sensuous line round her mouth with a caressing finger. He seemed to like the texture of her skin and the delicate shape of her ears. When she would have hidden her face from him, he tipped up her chin, boring into her with his eyes until she felt dizzy. Everything began going round and suddenly she was clinging to him, unable to either speak or move.

The height and breadth of him was formidable. He was strong but it wasn't just his strength which held her immobile. There was a strange heat coming from him, threatening, overpowering. It lit fires inside her, sending flames leaping through her veins, whipping every sluggish pulse to frantic action. Their breath intermingled as his eyes beat impatient, determined messages into hers, yet he made no attempt to kiss her or even hold her closer.

'Hear me again then,' he breathed, 'while your brave little soul shakes with fright. I'm not going to make love to you here. If I decide I want you, it will be when there is all the time in the world and the place is right.'

'You can't be serious!' she gasped. 'We've only met a few times.'

'It's the mixture of fire and ice that intrigues me,' he said softly. 'And the challenge.'

She closed her eyes against such cool insolence. His voice had the softness of a cobra's. She wasn't deceived.

'I only work for you. I can leave.'

'Somehow I don't think you're that much of a coward.'

She clenched her hands and nearly stopped trembling. 'Being sensible has nothing to do with being a coward.'

He put her firmly from him. 'But you won't.'

'Not unless I have to,' she felt her relief at being set free tempered by despair. Helplessly she appealed to him, 'Good jobs aren't easy to find.'

'Something you should perhaps keep in mind,' he murmured coolly, turning her back up the beach.

In London again, he asked where she lived, and, after finding her flat stopped outside it. 'I'm going back to the office,' he said, 'but you don't have to.'

Neale felt she should have done. Rex was away and there might be things which required her attention. It was a relief that Lawton didn't ask to come in though, or try to get over her doorstep by begging for a cup of coffee. That he had made no advances on the way home and now seemed eager to leave her, must be proof that he regretted the episode on the beach and was going to treat her as she wished to be treated, from now on?

She was dredging up a cool little smile of farewell when he said, 'I'm giving a party tomorrow evening, Neale. I'd like you to come.'

The smile dissolved in instant fright. 'Oh, I don't think so.'

'Why not?' he stared at her darkly, 'It's Saturday so you have no excuse. Unless you have another date?'

She would liked to have lied but shook her head. 'What kind of a party? Office?'

'No. It has nothing to do with the office,' he replied. 'Just a few friends. Will you come?'

Because he had thrown her hairpins away, her hair kept tumbling over her face and she tossed it back, meeting his eyes angrily, feeling trapped. 'I might.'

'You'd better,' he heard his teeth snap together. 'This isn't an invitation, Neale, it's an order! Be at my place, nine o'clock sharp,' he rapped out the address, 'unless you wish to be made redundant.'

The next night found Neale gazing unhappily at her reflection. She was going to Lawton's party but was still wondering why she had allowed herself to be threatened into it. That afternoon she had gone shopping for a new dress, which must be another regrettable sign of Lawton Baillie's increasing influence as it was something she hadn't done in a long time. There was nothing really wrong with the dresses already hanging in her wardrobe, so why was she so eager to impress him?

She choose a shop where the racks were full of all the latest fashions and exclusive enough to be quiet on a Saturday afternoon.

'Size ten?' the voice of the saleswoman purred in the ears of the browsing girl. 'Why not try the grey, Miss? It's a beautiful gown.'

Neale considered it carefully. 'I wonder?'

'Or, perhaps—black?' the woman assessed Neale expertly. 'You could really wear anything, Miss, with your figure. Are you a model?'

'No,' Neal replied absently, thinking it was just her luck to find someone determined to flatter her into buying something.

Yet when she tried on the black, almost backless as well as frontless, almost everything yet not quite anything, she gasped incredulously.

'Now, what did I tell you?' the saleslady crooned, 'Wasn't I right?'

Neale couldn't dispute it. The dress clung to her figure, enhancing it suggestively, but was much more decorous than it appeared to be at first glance. But still she hesitated. 'I'm not sure it's exactly what I want . . .?'

'It might have been designed specially for you,' the woman insisted, not always willing, or able to influence a customer against her will, but well able to deal with a little foolish wavering. 'I imagine you're going to a party? You'll certainly charm all the young men, wearing that.'

Which did the trick, if only because of the idea it somehow inserted in Neale's mind. She would go to Lawton's party and flirt madly with every man who came near her. Then Lawton might decide she was quite normal, after all, and forget about the therapeutic treatment he seemed to think she was in need of.

In the end, in a fit of wild extravagance, she bought a white dress as well as the black and returned home to wash her hair and decide which one she should wear? The crazy notions which had flashed through her head in the boutique had long since been severely dealt with, but, nevertheless, she settled for the black. Worn sedately, in it she might just pass unnoticed?

Lawton's penthouse wasn't difficult to find but was further away than she thought. Standing outside his door, after paying off the taxi, she despaired that she couldn't raise sufficient courage to ring the bell. Fortunately two other late arrivals came up behind her, leaving her with no alternative but to accompany them inside.

They seemed a nice enough couple, inclined to be friendly. At least the man was. He called her darling twice in as many minutes and kept touching her arm. Her new dress must be working like a charm, Neale thought, suppressing a giggle as the man's female companion glared at her and dragged him away.

Immediately they were gone Neale felt nervous again. Overwhelmed by a sense of panic, she turned to flee.

'Going somewhere?' Lawton asked suavely. ·

He entered the hall at the exact moment Neal turned. As she flushed scarlet and went rigid, he laughed, 'You look as guilty as a burglar caught in the act. What do I say? The game's up?'

Neale's eyes dilated to a cloudy grey as she poised to stare at him, all flying hair and fragile charm. She realised he was merely teasing, but somehow his words connected with something she was afraid of. Her feelings! While refusing to analyse them, she was aware that he could alter her heartbeats simply by looking at her. As he was doing now.

She mustn't let him guess though. His gibes might rankle but she must pretend not to be affected by anything he said or did. If she was only half alive, wasn't it better than enduring the uncertainty of being in love? Men were getting crueler every day, as their victims discovered to their cost! Women suffered, the innocent ones most, while men laughed at them for being so vulnerable.

Lawton was looking at her silently, not taking any notice of her silence. His eyes were wandering slowly over her, a journey of interest and appreciation. 'I like your hair and dress,' he said at last, 'black suits you and you should always wear your hair like that.'

'It wouldn't be practical,' she retorted shortly. Another woman might have parried his remarks with a coy glance and flirtatious reply but that was the best she could do. Wanted to do!

She stepped aside, her movements jerky. He might be enjoying studying her but she couldn't bring herself to look at him any longer. And you've only just arrived, a mocking voice whispered, but she ignored it.

He was magnificent. The thought crossed her mind with depressing frequency each time they met, but this evening he surpassed that description. She had never seen him dressed up before and the severity of formal evening clothes suited him. But his appearance didn't suit her! Her pulses began acting oddly, making her immediately wary.

'Here, let me take your wrap.'

Reaching for it, his hands lingered on her shoulders. 'You have a beautiful skin,' he murmured caressingly, 'I've never seen anything so perfect.' It wasn't until she trembled and stirred agitatedly, that he removed her wrap and tossed it to a hovering maid.

'Your—staff?' Neale gulped, her eyes dazedly following the white-capped figure.

'No. I don't have any living in. When I give a party a firm supplies everything, including staff. I'm away so much it wouldn't be worth having anyone here permanently.'

'Specially when you're not married.'

'How do you know I'm not?' he asked lightly.

'Oh,' she floundered, quite truthfully unable to answer, 'I suppose it's common knowledge.'

'Yes,' again his eyes went over her, 'I suppose it is. Somehow marriage has never appealed to me.'

Greatly daring, she exclaimed. 'You'd rather have a mistress?'

'They are certainly easier to get rid of,' he smiled mockingly, firmly taking hold of her arm. 'Shall we go in before my guests come looking for me?'

The reception rooms were large. Neale recognised no one. She might later. All she saw now was a sea of faces. She could tell by the glitter of jewellery, the fragrance of expensive perfume, the standard of dress, to what class most of Lawton's friends belonged, and, though she didn't feel inferior, she doubted if she would know a soul here.

Lawton was looking about him. 'I want you to meet someone,' he said. 'Come over here.'

Neale's heart sank. Who? He sounded as if he was speaking of someone special. And someone special could only be a woman.

He released her hand when he felt her withdrawal and grasped her elbow. Gently he pulled her along until, to her surprise, he stopped in front of a man.

'My brother, Freddy,' he said sardonically.

As he introduced her, Neale looked at Freddy curiously. He was nothing like Lawton. They were both dark but that was the only similarity. He wasn't nearly as tall or as broad as Lawton and he was younger.

'I shouldn't have guessed you were even related!'

While she blushed at having spoken her thoughts

aloud, Freddy laughed and explained, 'We're half-brothers, actually. Same mother but different fathers.'

Lawton might have warned her! She heard him saying with a kind of savage impatience. 'Where's June? I left her with you.'

Neale bit her lip as Freddy drawled carelessly. 'She's around.'

'Aren't you looking after her?'

'There are people paid to do that, old chap. Paid well!'

Neale glanced from one to the other in bewilderment. There was a distinct air of animosity between the two of them and she wondered, who is June? Some girl they both admired? June was the one, not Freddy, Neale suspected, whom Lawton was keen for her to meet, and she must be a fairly potent force if her absence could bring such a frown to his face?

Lawton might be anxious about June but Freddy didn't seem to be. Neale felt his eyes swing to her and liven with interest.

'Who are you?' he asked. 'No!' he held up his hand, 'don't tell me, let me guess. You're the new young actress Lawton met at Lyn's party last week. June said he was quite smitten. Or so she thought. Forgive me if I was sceptical of her description. I can see now she wasn't exaggerating. You're certainly something!'

'Neale is not an actress.' Lawton was amused.

Neale almost glared at him. Instead she managed a studied smile. Lawton wasn't responsible for a case of mistaken identity and he had every right to be smitten by as many stars as he liked!

Freddy looked quite peeved. 'You could have fooled me.' He glanced at his brother suspiciously, 'Are you sure she isn't? She has the face and figure. . . .'

'Freddy!' Lawton said firmly, 'cut it out. If Neale was an actress it would be no secret.'

Freddy reluctantly restrained his roving eyes. His rather weak mouth curled. 'Do you see, Neale, how he

orders me about? Ever since the day I was born he's
been doing it.'

'If it wasn't for June,' Lawton's voice hardened but
was interrupted by someone coming alongside him
asking sweetly, 'If it wasn't for what, darling?'

Lawton grinned down at her, ignoring her query.
'Where have you been? I wanted you to meet someone
and I've just been ticking your husband off for
neglecting you. This is Neale Curtis.'

'Actually I think I'm the one doing the neglecting,'
June laughed, as she shook Neale's hand, 'I left Freddy
to talk to some friends.'

June's hand was warm and soft, she seemed a nice
person, as well as beautiful and her explanation
sounded perfectly feasible. So why did Lawton not offer
his brother an apology, and why did Freddy throw his
wife such a derisive glance?

'I thought Miss Curtis was the actress you were
telling me about?' he said, after Lawton had got them
all drinks.

June smiled at Neale, her smile friendly. She gazed
more closely at the other girl's above average looks.
'You could be, of course, but you aren't.'

'Could we possibly let the subject drop?' Lawton
drawled. 'Neale happens to work for me as an interior
decorator.'

'Why, how marvellous!' June exclaimed, 'I'd never
have guessed.'

Freddy said, with a suggestive leer, 'You can come
and start on our place any day, darling. I'll even offer
to help. There,' ignoring Neale's startled face, he said to
Lawton, 'doesn't that please you, big brother? Aren't
you always telling me I should find something to do?'

Lawton muttered tersely. 'Shut up.'

'Why should I?' Freddy objected, downing his whisky
and grabbing another from a passing tray. 'I'm going to
ask Neale to dance and we can discuss when she might
begin.'

Neale swallowed, wondering what she had got herself into. But she needn't have worried. Lawton sighed and took hold of her hand again. 'Sorry, Freddy, I asked her first.' With a brief smile at June, he added, 'We will see you later.'

What was all that about? Neale wondered, not unhappy to escape. It was an odd situation and some of the remarks that had been made puzzled her. Why, for instance, should Lawton show such concern for his sister-in-law? She seemed a healthy enough individual, both in mind and body, so why should her husband talk of people being paid to look after her?

She found it difficult to believe that Lawton was in love with his brother's wife though there had been a caring look in his eyes when they had rested on her. He might have let his feelings for her develop dangerously without meaning to. June was a very attractive woman and obviously not indifferent to him.

On their way to another room, where a small band could be heard playing, they were stopped many times by people wishing to speak to Lawton. Neale had no chance to say she had no particular desire to dance, or to ask about his brother. He had a dazzling array of friends and introduced Neale to each one he paused to talk to, but she couldn't remember half their names. Being aware of the curious glances she was receiving didn't help her mind to function properly. She felt uncomfortable. Why did Lawton appear to be deliberately fostering the impression that she was someone special?

They reached the other room and he swung her on to the floor. She glanced at him anxiously, wanting to avoid such close contact with him yet perversely attracted to him. Desire lent a certain warmth to her skin, a betraying bonelessness to her body as she allowed herself to be drawn into his arms. Then realising what she was doing, she stiffened, searching for something to say that might sound more sensible than she was feeling.

'Your brother isn't like you.'

'He isn't?'

Neale tried again, 'He's younger.'

'By ten years, so is June.'

'I see.'

Lawton smiled down at her. 'I doubt if you do. I'll tell you about them later, if you're still interested.'

Which was one way of telling her it was none of her business. Neale quivered with resentment.

Lawton pulled her closer. 'Why can't you relax with me, Neale? Must you be always fighting? You always seem on the verge of taking flight.'

Neale's pulses began to race and she froze automatically. 'If I promise not to run away will you let me go?'

'That's beyond my intelligence to answer,' he teased. 'Either way I seem to lose.'

With his warm breath on her cheek, she trembled against him. 'Surely it wouldn't be the first time?'

'It might be the first time it mattered,' he growled.

She flushed, disliking him intensely. 'You aren't asking me to believe that?'

'I did say might,' he reminded her mildly.

'I didn't want to come here tonight,' she retorted sharply, her dislike increasing as she realised he was laughing at her, 'but not only did you use leverage by way of your position in order to get me here, you force me to dance with you. You'll be telling me next I deliberately encouraged your brother!'

He grinned. 'If you did, you were probably doing it unconsciously. That black dress is very provocative and you have lovely breasts.'

Gasping with outrage, colour ran up Neale's cheeks. 'That isn't true.'

His eyes darkened as his head bent threateningly nearer. 'I assure you it is.'

Neale's pulse gained speed as she endured his cool appraisal. Panic consumed her too. She was suddenly frantic to be free of him as she felt the wall of ice round her heart shaking. It mightn't be possible to fight him on his own ground but fight him she must!

A little desperately she said. 'Why don't you ask someone else to dance? You have a duty towards your guests.'

'You're one.'

'I'm merely an employee.'

'Not this evening,' his voice was seducingly low. 'Tonight neither of us need think of work. We're quite free to do as we like.'

Could there be anyone more devious! A soft little explosion of sound escaped her. 'If you give a party, you can't just turn your back on your obligations!'

'Will you stop gabbling!' he muttered darkly, his arms tightening until she was drawn against the whole length of him, his big body imposing itself on hers, making her aware of his strength as she had never been before, not even yesterday, on the beach. He actually hurt her, with the arm round her waist pressing her so firmly to the shape of his lower limbs that she felt her cheeks grow hot.

He took a handful of her gleaming masses of hair, twisting it in his fingers to stop her struggling. Painfully he pulled her head to his shoulder so he could avail himself of her neck and cheek. She held her breath in a state of frozen enthralment as his mouth moved sensitively over her skin. He sighed contentedly, moulding her to him then quite sharply bit her ear.

The quick pain sent fright spilling through her. Incoherently, her mind reeling, Neale gasped. 'Please, Lawton, that hurt!'

'Only that?' his laughter was low against it. 'Would you rather I bit somewhere else?'

Neale shivered, her cheeks bright red, 'I don't have to listen to remarks like that.'

There was a glow in his eyes. 'My beautiful girl, where's your sense of humour?'

She said coldly, 'Not on the same wavelength as yours, apparently.'

'You can say that again,' he looked at her more soberly. 'Most women enjoy this kind of thing.'

'Maybe the kind of women you know,' she acceded, far from graciously. 'And don't tell me again,' she flared, 'if I don't change my tune I'll end up an old maid. I just don't happen to need or want a man!'

'You're issuing a very dangerous challenge,' he said softly.

'I'm not issuing anything,' she stated flatly. 'I'm merely expressing a wish to be left alone.'

He smiled and without replying bent his head to let his mouth crush her lips. She moaned, feeling herself lost, unable to stop the tide of passion that came rushing from nowhere to drown her. It only lasted a few seconds but even that fleeting, ion of time managed to transform her completely. She felt herself lift on her toes as he pressed her closer, her mouth clinging as hungrily as his.

When he stopped kissing her she was forced to go on clinging to him to hide her embarrassment. 'I—what will people think?' she stammered.

'It doesn't matter,' he said calmly.

His coolness horrified her. 'You didn't have to try and prove anything,' she said bitterly. 'I told you it was no contest.'

He stared at her narrowly. 'Every time you look at me, Neale, you provoke me. Don't tell me you don't know it.'

'I don't,' she insisted.

He saw the strain on her face and felt her trembling. 'I think we will postpone this discussion until later, when everyone has gone.'

Neale intended being the first to leave but didn't say so. With a wrench of anger she withdrew from his arms and asked to be directed to the cloakroom.

Smiling ironically he not only directed her but

escorted her there himself. She took the pleasure of perhaps childishly slamming the door in his face and wished it was made of glass so she might have seen his expression.

She managed to refresh herself by rinsing her hands and cheeks under the cold tap and used a little make-up to repair the damage. If she could have done, she would have left straight away but when she emerged from the cloakroom she saw Lawton standing by the front door, talking to a group of people, with his eyes daring her to try and get past him.

Dejectedly she returned to the reception rooms where, to her relief, June waved for her to join her. Freddy was nowhere to be seen and with Lawton in the hall, she felt able to relax for the first time since she had arrived.

'I tell you what,' June suggested, 'why don't we have some coffee sent to Lawton's study? He won't mind and the noise here's making me dizzy.'

Gratefully, Neale agreed. Lawton had introduced her to plenty of people but she didn't feel she knew anyone well enough to talk to and she was getting tired of the curious glances increasingly thrown in her direction.

Lawton's study was big and quiet, with a feeling of being remote from the rest of the house. A maid brought coffee and she poured it out while June arranged half-a-dozen dreamy records on the stereo.

'Ah, that's better!' she smiled, flinging herself down in a low chair opposite Neale and reaching for a sandwich.

'Won't Freddy be missing you?' Neale asked uncertainly.

June laughed, rather mirthlessly. 'No. He's busy propping up the bar. He's likely to be there until we leave, when Lawton will dump him in a taxi.'

Neale glanced at her curiously. She had been glad to come in here but in other circumstances she might have enjoyed dancing and mixing with the crowd. And she had cleaned her flat today as well as washing and shopping. June, on the other hand, apparently did nothing, yet she sounded exhausted.

The music flowed about them, very soothing. With a sigh June sank back and closed her eyes.

Neale asked uncertainly, recalling how concerned Lawton had been, 'Are you feeling all right?'

She didn't know how she had expected June to answer but was startled when she exclaimed lightly, 'As all right as most women feel, I suppose, in the first stages of pregnancy.'

'You're pregnant?' Neale smiled warmly, and many things now became clear to her. 'Why, how lovely. I expect you're delighted?'

'Yes,' June sighed wearily. 'At least I think I'm delighted. I know I definitely was when I first learnt what was happening to me.'

'So,' Neale frowned, 'what's the problem? I mean, apart from not feeling too good.'

'It's Freddy,' June hesitated then plunged on bitterly, 'you'd think he would be but he isn't a bit pleased!'

CHAPTER THREE

NEALE's eyes widened with a surprise she couldn't immediately hide. She didn't know what to say. She was aware that people often told strangers things they wouldn't dream of mentioning to their nearest and dearest but she wished June had told her about the baby and not Freddy.

'I believe some husbands do feel less than pleased in the beginning,' she said awkwardly. 'In fact, I remember Mummy once telling me that my father wasn't too thrilled to learn I was on the way. He confessed later he was jealous.'

'Really?' June looked thoughtful. 'I—well, I've thought of that, of course, but most husbands are jealous because they love their wives too much. With Freddy it's a case of loving himself too much. He never wants to share the limelight. He has an insatiable desire for it, you see.'

Neale felt not a little embarrassed. June was determined to tell her things she had no wish to hear and she might regret such confidences later. But how to stop her without seeming rude or unsympathetic?

'Is your husband in the same business as Lawton?' she asked, hoping to divert June gently from her concentration on the baby, as obviously her husband's antipathy towards it was causing her distress.

June's brows rose wryly. 'Didn't you hear Freddy complaining how Lawton is always advising him to find something to do?'

'Yes, but I didn't take it seriously,' Neale frowned. 'Doesn't everyone have to do something, nowadays, to live?'

'Most people,' June agreed, adding curiously, 'Lawton doesn't appear to have told you much?'

'I only work for him,' Neale said gently, believing, if she reminded June of this, she might stop talking about his family.

June didn't, 'It's no secret, so you don't have to worry,' she said. 'Lawton's stepfather was in his sixties when Freddy was born and was so delighted with the only child he had managed to sire that he went out immediately and bequeathed him all his wordly goods, which weren't inconsiderable. Perhaps he meant to change his will later but he never did. Freddy was twenty when he died and inherited more money than was good for him.'

'Didn't Lawton mind?'

'If he did it never showed.'

Neale's brow furrowed as, against her will the story intrigued her. 'So your husband has never actually needed to work?'

'Unfortunately, no,' June said tightly.

'And Lawton . . .?'

'Fought his way up from the bottom. He had a little money left to him by his own father but not enough to make an appreciable difference. He is where he is today through sheer hard work and intelligence although I've heard him refer to it as being lucky.'

Neale sighed. And she had imagined he'd been born with a silver spoon in his mouth! 'How does he and your husband get on?'

'Do call him Freddy. Amazingly well in some ways, not at all in others. Lawton tends to come down with a heavy hand when Freddy steps out of line.'

'Doesn't Freddy mind?'

June grimaced. 'He's used to it—relies on it, I sometimes think.'

'And you?'

This time June smiled warmly. 'I could never complain. Lawton's always very good to me. There are times when I wished I loved him instead of Freddy. Not that it might have done me much good,' her expression was wry again, 'Lawton enjoys women but I doubt if he will every marry. He treasures his freedom too much.'

Neale had no wish to delve into that aspect of Lawton's life. Anyway, it was none of her business. 'How long have you been married?' she asked slowly.

'Five years. We were both twenty-three. Freddy perhaps was too young and it hasn't been easy. This was why I hoped the baby might make a difference.'

'I'm sure it will do,' Neale encouraged warmly. 'It's early days yet, and,' she crossed her fingers against the white lie, 'he does seem concerned for you.'

'You think so?' June's eyes suddenly glowed eagerly, 'They do say outsiders often see most. Oh, forgive me!' she exclaimed, 'but you know what I mean.'

Neale nodded guiltily but returned June's warm smile. The other girl was so easy to like and so charming it was nearly impossible to believe she had anything but an adoring husband.

June yawned and reached for more coffee. 'Do you know, I feel better already. I'm so used to telling Lawton everything but I find it easier to talk to another woman about my baby.' Her glance sharpened curiously. 'You might have one yourself, one day. Why aren't you married?'

'I'm concentrating on my career,' Neale replied stiffly.

'Does Lawton let you?' June asked innocently.

Neale flushed. 'I don't follow. I work for him—he has to.'

'That wasn't what I meant,' June's mood was suddenly teasing, 'I saw the way he looked at you. I'm still trying to come up with some conclusions.'

'I'm not really interested in men,' Neale assured her quickly.

'Not even men like my brother-in-law?' June laughed dryly, then, taking mercy on Neale's hot face, apologised lightly and began discussing the record being played.

No one came near and Mendelssohn proved very soothing. Neale didn't remember falling asleep and when she woke it took her a few seconds to get her bearings. Until she saw Lawton stretched lazily in the chair where June had been, she thought she was back in her own flat. Discovering she wasn't was almost as great a shock as discovering it was well after midnight.

Lawton was looking at her, his glance travelling slowly down the length of her, making her suddenly realise she was lying on the couch.

'I'm sure I wasn't like this!' she gasped, swinging her feet to the floor.

'Hush!' Lawton laughed, 'You've committed no crime. When I came searching for you, you were sound asleep and June thought it might be kinder to leave you. I simply made you more comfortable.'

Neale furtively slid her feet into her sandals. 'You should have woken me up.'

'You might not have been more appreciative than you are now!' he chided sardonically.

She made an effort to control her temper. 'I don't usually fall asleep when I'm asked out. I'm sorry.'

He contemplated her idly for a moment. 'June shouldn't have burdened you with her troubles.'

'I didn't mind,' Neale looked at him uncertainly from under thick lashes. 'She didn't say much.'

'Enough to make you miss the party.'

'It wasn't her fault I fell asleep,' she exclaimed. 'And the party's irrelevant. It's more important that I should be home. Where can I ring for a taxi?'

He rose to his feet and pushed her down again as she jumped to hers. 'You aren't going anywhere until you've had some coffee and sandwiches. Then I'll take you home myself.'

'I don't want anything,' she protested, 'I'm not hungry.'

'You're too thin.'

'It's fashionable.'

He sat down beside her with a sigh. 'You probably work too hard.'

'I'm sure you're right,' she tried to joke about it, 'you're a slave-driver.'

'I hope not,' he frowned as if he was really considering it. 'Take your time over the south coast job. I don't want you wearing yourself out.'

'I'm sure I'm not irreplaceable,' she retorted, wondering how she could speak so flippantly with her heart racing in unaccountable panic.

'For me you might be,' he said calmly.

She laughed hollowly, not believing him for a second. He could have any woman he liked. He didn't have to pretend he was interested in Neale Curtis.

He moved closer, his hands moving to her face. The blood rushed through her veins, vividly colouring her cheeks and altering her breathing. As he cupped her chin, he murmured probingly, 'I don't know what the man you were once engaged to did to you, Neale, but he certainly dented your self-confidence. He appears to have taken your spirit, along with everything else.'

'Tony didn't. . . .'

'So that's his name. I don't like it.'

'What's in a name?' she whispered, her voice strained, 'Tony and I were finished years ago. He just left me hating men.'

'You're going to change your mind about me though. Aren't you, Neale?'

'No,' she gasped, immediately recognising danger. 'Never!'

Lawton laughed low in his throat. 'You're a beautiful girl, Neale, and I don't believe in waste.'

'I'm not beautiful . . .!'

'There you go again,' he took a handful of her hair, 'Look at this, masses of it, shining, lustrous silk and the colour's fantastic. As are your eyes. They're mauve or green, sometimes a stormy sky grey, depending on your mood.'

'Lawton, please . . .!'

'Be quiet. I've only just got started.' He turned her face, his hands caressing the smooth skin and she couldn't look at him. Overwhelmed by shyness she lowered her eyes until her lashes lay curled against her cheeks. 'Look at me, Neale,' he said, and when she wouldn't he placed a finger under her chin.

'All right then,' he murmured. 'I was going to tell you about your mouth but if you won't listen perhaps I can make you aware of it in a different way?'

His arms came round her, enfolding her, drawing her close to his hard frame. Neale went tense, her slight body trembling as she tried to fight his strength and the deep spell he seemed to be deliberately weaving about her.

Gathering every scrap of resolve she could find, she did her best to escape him. 'Why are you tormenting me like this?' she cried. 'Is it some new game? Why don't you ring your actress friend or one of the dozens of other women you know? You can't possibly want me.'

'Can't I?' he said roughly, his mouth covering hers with an urgency she couldn't deny. Her senses began to reel as he kissed her and she clung to him helplessly, forgetting about fighting him. As before, she found the deliberateness of his approach unbearably exciting. She might protest forever but she knew she had been secretly aching to have him kiss her.

She made one last attempt. 'Lawton, please let me go.'

'Why? When we both want the same thing?' His mouth made a thorough tour of her neck, nibbling in a painfully gentle way that left Neale breathless with longing.

When he reached the cleft between her breasts and his hands pushed the delicate fabric aside to reveal one rose-tipped mound, she gave an inarticulate little cry. Her hands clutched at him convulsively as she tried to summons the resolution which was swiftly fading.

'Stop fighting, darling. Forget about your career.

This won't interfere with it anyway. It might even help.'

'No!' Neale gasped, closing her eyes as his hands cupped her breasts, stroking and caressing. Waves of the wildest sensation washed over her making her voice shake.

'You've denied yourself too long,' he told her, even his voice sending ripples of heat right through her. 'You're lovely,' he murmured, his warm mouth closing over a taut nipple, shooting her into a state of sensuous shock. By the time he raised his head to take possession of her parted lips and carry her through to his bedroom she was so consumed by frantic longing that she wasn't able to utter even a single murmur of protest.

He carried her over to the bed and put her down gently. As the softness of the bed enfolded her, her eyes flew open but before she could begin to reproach him, he was down beside her, his arms around her again, expertly silencing her.

What was she doing? she wondered dimly, as he soothed her gently and like a well-trained puppet her body arched towards him. She knew she should leave him but was unable to do so. As Lawton's hands calmed her, burning a path through her defences, she closed her eyes and tried not to tremble. When his lips forced hers apart, seeking entry for his tongue which began exploring, she responded convulsively to his demanding passion.

She was submerged in a pool of sensuous delight, not even realising when he began undressing her. Her zipper moved silently, her dress sliding away with his shirt and her softness was pressed against the hardness of his bare chest.

He held her close, kissing her eyelids, sending her into spasms of rapture. She ought to tell him she was a virgin, but having got this far she couldn't bear the thought of his anger. He must be used to an experienced partner, if he learnt she was completely innocent he might be furious.

He kissed the corner of her mouth, feeling it part to his seeking lips, drawing his breath sharply at this sure sign of her surrender. Laying her back against the pillows, his eyes smouldered over her, his hands spreading out on her body, his long fingers almost able to span her waist. Almost reverently he traced the smooth skin on her slender hips and flat stomach before removing her bra. As the wisp of silk disappeared, leaving her covered by only the briefness of her lacy panties, he murmured softly, 'You're beautiful, my darling, and I want every inch of you.'

His eyes devoured her and Neale shivered before the flames in them. Her arms lifted to his neck and she groaned, unable to stop the tide of desire which was rushing to drown her.

Lawton's mouth touched hers gently then became relentlessly passionate. His practised caresses brought mounting excitement and when he took first one then the other taut nipple in his mouth, she gasped, relinquishing her last threads of sanity. Involuntarily her nails dug fiercely in the muscled hardness of his shoulders and a helpless cry escaped her.

As his fingers pushed carefully into the top of her panties and he eased them slowly over her trembling limbs, she was consumed by impatience. With his hands stealing along her skin, she pressed against him, her mouth clinging hungrily to his, feeling herself dissolving in flames she couldn't control. When at last she lay in his arms, naked, there was a fire burning between them impossible to put out.

With his mouth still pressed to hers, Lawton reached for his belt and Neale could only cling to him, dazed with passion. The knowledge that he shared this passion and that it was driving him to possess her ruthlessly, did nothing to dilute the fever of her own response.

How long the doorbell had been ringing. Neale had no idea. Its penetrating tones broke through the drugged inertia gripping her, like the knell of doom.

'Lawton!' she gasped, 'Someone must want you.'

His startled eyes met her dazed ones. 'It must be three o'clock!'

'Still early for London,' she reminded him breathlessly.

'Forget it,' he said tersely, lowering himself down on her again. 'They can go to hell.'

The ringing continued. 'You'll have to go and see,' Neale felt suddenly cold. 'It could be the police or someone in trouble.'

'Oh, God!' he rolled from her off the bed, his face dark with anger, 'I suppose I must, but whoever is there had better have a good excuse, or I might just kill them!'

Retrieving a robe from a cupboard, he belted it on as he strode through the door. 'Stay there, darling,' he commanded Neale, 'I'll be right back.'

The coldness which had attacked Neale when the bell rang, grew worse and was joined by an increasing feeling of horror. She began to shake as she realised what she had been about to surrender. For years she had striven to recoup her self-respect. Tony had taken most of it and she had been going to hand what remained of it to another man who wouldn't hesitate to treat her as badly as he had!

Cursing herself for being a fool, she scrambled hastily into her dress. Carefully, for she was still shaking, she eased the bedroom door slightly. There was a woman in the hall, a voluptuous redhead, clearly hysterical, hanging on to Lawton's arm. She was sobbing something about loosing a valuable diamond earring at the party, and how Brian—whom Neale presumed was her husband—would murder her if she didn't recover it!

Where was Brian?

'Home, asleep,' the voice, more coy now than hysterical, answered Lawton's curt question.

They disappeared into the lounge, where Neale guessed from Lawton's tone, the search for the missing earring would be brief. Swiftly, like a small, hunted animal, she let herself out of the apartment and hailed a taxi. She remembered little of being driven home as she spent the half-hour journey struggling to rid her mind of pictures she had no wish to see.

As soon as she entered her flat Neale stripped off her dress and dived under the shower. Somehow she felt less than clean, a feeling she hadn't known since the last time Tony had touched her. She was determined to scrub away the feeling of Lawton's hands, and, she hoped, glancing reluctantly at the red marks on her skin, all evidence of her own folly.

She was busy drying herself when the phone rang and she was tempted to ignore it. It could only be Lawton and she had nothing to say to him. Then it struck her that he might be ringing to make sure she had got home safely, and if she didn't answer he might come looking. Chewing her bottom lip uneasily she decided it would be easier to speak to him over the phone. She had no wish to face him and she could imagine him breaking her door in if he arrived here and she pretended she wasn't in.

'Yes?' she yawned, seeking to give the impression that she had been asleep.

'Neale! Where the hell did you get to?' Lawton sounded more worried than angry. 'Why did you leave?'

It was a good thing she had, the way her body was responding to the mere sound of his voice! 'I'm sorry,' she replied, trying to stop trembling. 'Look, Lawton, I'm in bed and I'm tired, so I'll leave you to your redhead . . .!'

'Neale,' he interrupted quietly, 'I'm sorry. I'm as frustrated as you are but Evonne is the wife of an old friend and, much as I'd have liked to, I couldn't very well throw her out.'

'Did you find the earring?' Neale asked sarcastically.

'No, darling,' he added softly. 'Shall I come round?'

'No!' her voice rose in panic. 'Definitely not!'

'Spend the day with me tomorrow, Neale?' he pleaded huskily. 'Let me make up for your disappointment.'

He had a nerve! 'No!' she repeated, crashing down the receiver and ignoring it when it began ringing again. Lawton had put her through enough. Tonight had been unfortunate, putting it mildly. She needed time to rebuild her defences if she wasn't to see them, in their weakened state, completely demolished.

When eventually the telephone subsided, leaving a silence which seemed to hold a threat, Neale threw herself down on her bed, burying her hot face in a pillow. Lawton had managed to get under her guard, he had persuaded her into his arms and her foolish body had betrayed her. Fiercely she tried to deaden the still hot embers of desire. How could she still want a man to whom she was only a game? Something about her dedication to her career, a few things she had inadvertently let drop regarding her past had obviously caught his imagination, but what would happen to his interest, once she had given in to him? It would disappear, as soon as she stopped resisting him. Which might leave her in a worse state than she had been after being deserted by Tony. Tony she had successfully walled out but Lawton was a much stronger character. He might not be nearly so easy to forget as Tony. With a contemptuous groan for her own stupidity, Neale turned over and tried to get some sleep.

It must have been a long time in coming for next morning she slept in and to her dismay she was awakened by the phone. It kept on ringing and with a sigh of defeat she got out of bed and dressed. Quickly she left the flat, without bothering about breakfast. Judging from the strident ringing of the telephone, Lawton was determined to contact her and if she stayed in she might not be able to avoid him.

She spent the day exploring parts of London she hadn't seen in years and returned home pleasantly

exhausted. Her two small rooms were silent. There was
no indication that anyone had been trying to contact
her. The door hadn't been knocked down, nor had a
note been pushed through it. Lawton must have given
up. Neale thought of this uncertainly for a moment
then gave a sigh of relief. His absence mightn't prove a
lot but it did seem to indicate he was a man who could
take a hint.

The following morning, when she reached the office,
Neale was disconcerted to discover Rex wouldn't be
back for another day or two. He'd been in touch with
Mildred, who coped with the department's secretarial
work, and she relayed his message.

'He sounds busy,' she said flippantly. 'He didn't say
what with.'

'You're sure he said just a day or two?' Neale
frowned, having expected to be able to consult him as
soon as she came in.

'That's what he said,' Mildred sang out blithely. 'He
said you were to carry on.'

He would! Neale flung off her mac and adjusted her
hair pins bitterly. Her trip to the south coast hotel with
Lawton might have been constructive but she couldn't
really do much without Rex's permission. Her visit to
the hotel might have thrown up fresh possibilities but
vision was a mixture of illusion and reality. In this case
she had perceived several changes that might be made
without much difficulty but she needed help in trying to
interpret them.

Sitting down at her desk she began making some
study models from heavy drafting paper. Lawton's
interference had merely confused the issue. Now they
had to co-opt his ideas with their own and it wouldn't
be easy. Rex and she had already discovered this before
he'd been whipped off to Spain. It wasn't just a matter
of changing the colour of a few rooms. With a sigh she
glanced at the bubble diagrams pinned on the drawing
boards. Each bubble represented spaces which rep-

resented rooms, and the designer must consider the overall arrangement, the visual effect of the whole, not just an individual apartment.

When Lawton rang she shook her head at Mildred, who, being quick-witted, murmured coolly, 'I'm afraid she's not in, sir. Where? Oh, I think she has just popped out.'

Looking puzzled, Mildred laid down the phone. 'He sounds a bit impatient. Don't you think it might have been wiser to speak to him?'

'He knows nothing can be finalised until Rex comes home,' Neale retorted crossly. 'Are you sure it wasn't Rex he asked for? He might have forgotten he's away.'

'No, he wanted you,' Mildred said emphatically, 'And he wants you to ring him as soon as you are in!'

Neale couldn't believe Lawton had put as much emphasis on those last two words as Mildred did but her stomach squirmed uneasily. What could Lawton wish to speak to her about? Work-wise he must know there was nothing fresh to report, so it could only be Saturday night. Her heart thudded, missing beats. She had thought he was a man who when frustrated would turn to someone else. Could it be she was wrong?

She worked through lunch for it hadn't been a good morning. When the phone rang, as she was alone in the department, she absently reached for it and picked it up. To her horror, she discovered it was Lawton.

'Oh, hello,' she gulped, striving to recover her composure.

'Neale!' he said curtly. 'Where on earth have you been? I've been trying to reach you.'

'I was busy,' she replied quickly. 'But I've nothing to show you that you haven't seen already.'

'I shouldn't mind another look.'

'Please!' at his teasing tones, a flush flooded her whole body.

'Have dinner with me, this evening?' Lawton laughed softly, as if he could actually see her hot cheeks and confused expression. 'Better still meet me for lunch. You can't have had yours yet.'

'I have,' her glance fell on the remains of a sandwich. 'Dinner then?'

'I'm sorry,' she murmured, 'I have things to do.'

'Another evening?' he suggested silkily and she tensed at the dangerous note in his voice.

It took a lot of courage to refuse.

'I'm not going down on my knees, Neale,' the cool tones became icy. 'You have your own reasons for refusing but make sure they're the right ones. I won't ask again.'

Neale waited until she was sure her voice was steady. 'The answer remains the same, Mr Baillie.'

The rasp of his breath came clearly. 'Neale! Didn't the other evening mean anything to you?'

'It was a strange evening, from beginning to end,' she choked.

'The end being even stranger than the beginning,' Lawton observed sarcastically. 'I presume your above-average performance in bed was merely pretence?'

'I—I'd rather not talk about it,' Neale stammered, feeling hot all over.

'I'd advise you to pause and consider before you lead a man on and change your mind again,' he taunted. 'Next time there might be no doorbell to save you.'

Stung, she cried, 'I couldn't arrange that!'

'No, but you forced me to answer it,' he retorted with soft savagery, 'Had it been left to me, it could have rang all night. Next time. . . .'

'There won't be a next time!' she gasped.

'Not with you,' he agreed, quietly cutting her off.

Neale worked so hard during the ensuing days, trying to forget Lawton Baillie and all he had said, that she began loosing weight and developed deep shadows under her eyes. It distressed her further that she achieved little to justify such increased activity. Nothing came out right. Try as she might, in several instances she just couldn't get the effect she strove for. Sometimes she felt she was a colour-blind idiot who had never been one of the star pupils of her year. Lawton's harsh features came between everything she did, imposing themselves on her mind until she began feeling haunted. He even invaded her dreams so she had no peace, even when asleep.

She was at a stage when she might have welcomed any diversion but when one arrived she was filled with dismay rather than pleasure. One morning, after picking up the telephone, Mildred placed a hand over the mouthpiece and giggled. 'It's for you, Neale. Mr Right, at last!'

Neale glanced up sharply, not in the mood for hilarity of any sort. 'Can't you see I'm busy, Mildred? Is this some joke?'

'Scouts' honour—or guides'!' Mildred giggled again, 'Said I'm to tell you it's Mr Right. If anyone's having a joke, it's him!' as she handed over the receiver, she prodded it meaningly with her finger.

Neale went several shades paler as she suddenly realised whom her mysterious caller might be. Her ex-fiancé's name was Wright, not spelt in the same way as Mildred used it but sounding the same. However could she have forgotten, even for a moment! It might be a coincidence, but she doubted it.

'Tony?' she murmured tentatively, taking over from Mildred with shaking hands.

'You took your time!' he complained. 'I thought you were refusing to speak to me.'

'I'm busy,' she faltered, feeling winded, 'and,' she saw thankfully that Mildred had been called to the other side of the room, 'I didn't realise who it was.'

'Well, never mind. How are you?' he laughed breezily, as if he had never jilted her and they'd never been apart.

'I'm fine,' she replied woodenly, not revealing that her very foundations were shaking.

'I've missed you, Neale.'

'How is your wife?' she asked coldly.

'I suppose I deserved that,' he muttered sulkily.

Impatiently she enquired, 'Where are you?' the last time she had heard of him he had been abroad.

'In London, for a conference,' he replied, with a familiar note of self-importance, 'I'm representing the firm.'

That would make Tony feel good. Neale's soft mouth tightened scornfully but she was glad it didn't seem to matter anymore.

'Can I see you?' he asked eagerly.

Neale hesitated, having lost all desire to see him.

'Come on, Neale,' he pleaded, when she didn't reply, 'take pity on me.'

Had he ever had any pity for her? The question went unasked as he wheedled some more, 'If you refuse to see me, I might jump in the Thames!'

Did he imagine she would care! The conceit of men— all men! never failed to astonish her. 'All right,' she gave in reluctantly, 'perhaps tomorrow.'

'Fine!' he laughed happily, 'Lunch. 'Where?'

'The Grosvenor?' she named the first place to enter her head. It was where she had lunched with Lawton and she hoped Tony would say it was too expensive. In the old days she had known him back off from a bun in a snack bar!

Apparently his circumstances had changed, she doubted that he had! 'That sounds great,' he agreed.

She was unable to resist murmuring. 'Are you sure you can afford it?'

'Of course!' he replied smugly. 'I'm not a poor man now, Neale.'

Neale could think of only one reason for having consented to have lunch with Tony, and that was to make sure her love for him was dead. But because she was already almost certain of this, she found herself regretting her impulsive decision to go out with him. When Lawton left word that he wanted to see her, early that afternoon, she felt that Fate was definitely working against her!

She found him on the top floor, where she believed chairmen and directors usually preferred to work, but this was only the second time Neale had ever been this high and she had never been in Lawton's office before. Despite her apprehension at being summoned by him at such short notice, she glanced around with interest.

His secretary showed her in. He was sitting behind a huge, polished desk which commanded a great deal of floor space. Neale gazed at it with considerable awe. Lawton thought big in everything, apparently, which must be half the secret of his success.

Feeling lost amidst such impressive surroundings, she raised reluctant eyes to his face, 'You wished to see me, Mr Baillie?'

'So we've decided to be formal, have we?' he had glanced up as she entered, now he leaned back in his chair, watching her mockingly.

'In working hours, I should have thought you'd prefer it?' she replied stiffly.

'It might be more honest to say you would, Miss Curtis,' he studied her dryly for a few taut seconds before barking abruptly. 'Well, sit down!'

She obeyed with relief, as a current of electricity vibrated between them, making her shake. Waiting for him to inform her as to why he wished to see her, she kept her eyes on the floor. This way she found she could control the speed of her pulse better than when she was looking at him but it didn't help her to forget how she had felt when she had been in his arms.

It wasn't until he revealed that Rex was delayed in Spain that her eyes met his again with a flash of alarm.

'How—long?'

'I can't say,' he replied vaguely. 'Problems have arisen which makes it sense for him to be there for at least another week.'

'I see.'

'Are you able to carry on without him?' he asked, observing her uncertainty.

'Of course,' Neale snapped, then flushed bright red as she realised this was no way to speak to her boss, especially if she hoped to continue working for him! 'I—I'm sorry,' she apologised hastily, 'I didn't mean to sound impertinent.'

'I wonder.' Dark blue eyes with a hint of steel lanced meditatively into her. 'Well? Have you any particular problems? How are the new colour schemes coming along? Have you anything fresh ready to show me?'

CHAPTER FOUR

LAWTON'S queries were quite straightforward so why did she feel there was more behind them than there appeared to be?

'It's rather difficult to make any definite decisions with Mr Fuller away,' she confessed uneasily. 'There are limits to the adjustments I can make without his authority.'

'Aren't you familiar with his—graphic language, isn't it called?'

She knew what he meant. 'Yes and no,' she replied carefully.

'I imagine his is inclined to be more traditional than yours,' Lawton said astutely. 'But since I've made my wishes clear on certain points and instructed you on how to carry them out, I can't see him rejecting anything you do.'

'It's not just that,' she protested. 'I do trust my own judgment and so does Rex, but in a job like this there are so many things to consider.'

'Such as?'

How could he expect her to condense in a few short sentences that which had taken years of training and experience to learn?

'Hundreds of things,' she didn't think she was exaggerating. 'Take light, for instance. I'm not familiar with every aspect of it, in the hotel. You must realise how it produces visual sensation, how, more basically, different lighting, even the strength of it, affects colour? And we have to get it right, this time, you said so yourself!'

He nodded, then startled her by saying. 'You might not have Rex immediately available but you could consult me. I may not possess his particular qualifications but I studied art for two years at night classes. It was a long time ago, in the days when I was willing to learn anything I thought might come in useful.'

'A—a lot of people like to dabble in art,' she said uncertainly.

'I did more than dabble, Neale,' he looked at her coldly. 'Bring whatever you're doing to me and I'll give you my opinion.'

Neale still wasn't sure what to make of his suggestion, but was she in any position to argue? Swallowing the protests rising in her throat, she asked awkwardly, 'Would it be possible for you to come to the studios? There's really too much to bring up here.'

'Bring what you can,' he said curtly. 'Tomorrow, just before noon will do nicely. That will be all, Miss Curtis.'

Lawton's sudden coldness, though not entirely unexpected, made Neale so unhappy that between thinking of him and Tony, she spent a miserable night. Yet Tony didn't occupy her thoughts anywhere near the same extent as Lawton did, and this, in itself, made her uneasy. Tony might have disturbed her by his sudden reappearance in her life but the relief that he hadn't the power to hurt her anymore was still there. In the morning she actually forgot all about him until she reached Lawton's office, laden with all the paraphernalia of her trade, when she suddenly remembered she had arranged to meet him at one.

Her date with Tony had gone right out of her head, and while in one respect she might have been pleased at the implications of this, in another it filled her with dismay. What was Lawton going to say when he learned she must leave almost as soon as she arrived?

'Come in, Neale.' He was working, but he glanced up with a smile as she staggered towards him.

He seemed in a good mood. Carefully she arranged some large carboard boxes where she hoped no one would trip over them. 'I had to bring my models,' she explained.

'Leave it for now,' he dismissed her efforts impatiently. 'Later will do. I'm sure we shall both feel more like working after a bite of lunch.'

'Lunch?' her eyes widened in consternation and she flushed.

'Don't say you've never heard of it?' he laughed, leaving his desk to come and stand beside her, letting his eyes rove intimately over her, 'You could do with some food, you're far too thin.'

Neale's flush deepened, changing from one of guilt to embarrassment. He had told her she was thin before and she sensed, from the glow in his eyes, that he was reminding her of that other occasion. And that was something she only wished to forget!

Angrily, she asked, 'What time will you be back from lunch?' She refused to believe he was inviting her to join him.

'That depends,' he smiled. 'We'll worry about that later.'

'We . . .?'

'You're coming with me.'

'Oh,' Neale could feel herself growing cold, 'I'm afraid I can't.'

'Can't.'

Did he have to snap, just like that! Her voice cooled defiantly. 'I've already arranged to go out.'

'I see,' there was frost in his eyes, 'Am I allowed to ask who with?'

'I don't see why not,' angrily she tilted her chin. 'With an old friend.'

'Who shall be nameless?'

She flinched at his sarcasm but stood her ground. 'His name would make no difference.'

'So it's a man,' he said smoothly. 'That much I'd already guessed, and I suppose the secrecy means that he's married? It's a game women enjoy playing, these days.'

Colour ran up Neale's cheeks. 'It isn't like that!' she retorted sharply. 'Tony is married but. . . .'

He was on it in a flash. 'So it's your ex-fiancé whom you're lunching with. I could never forget a name like that.'

'It's perfectly respectable,' she exclaimed, 'and we will only be talking over old times.'

'I thought you wanted to forget them?' he jeered.

'I have no particular desire to remember them,' she agreed evenly, 'but Tony is over here on a short visit from Canada, and when he rang and asked me out I could hardly refuse.'

'Just study the way you refuse me,' Lawton gibed. 'Then you should be able to say no to him very easily, next time.'

There wouldn't be a next time but she didn't tell Lawton this. She had already explained far too much that was really none of his business. If he was annoyed because she had so far declined to go out with him, then it was just too bad! She wasn't going to risk putting her emotions on a rack again, not for any man!

'I'll be back about two,' she murmured, wondering how she was going to manage it.

She turned, but found his hands on her shoulders, holding her still. 'Where are you lunching?' he grated.

'The—the Grosvenor,' she confessed, knowing she must have been crazy ever to think of it.

'Why there?' he stared at her curiously, his breath cool on her face.

Neale stirred, her flesh tingling under his hands, her mind confused by desires that had nothing to do with either lunch or Tony.

Hollowly she replied, 'I don't really know.'

'Was it your suggestion?'

When she nodded, he said acidly. 'I'll tell you why. You're taking your old boyfriend there so you can exorcise his ghost as well as mine. It's called killing two birds with one stone.'

'Now you're being ridiculous!' she cried, afraid of the truth even when Lawton put it to her bluntly. 'Tony isn't familiar with London and I was really too busy to talk to him when he rang. I suggested the Grosvenor as it was the first place to enter my head. Perhaps because I had been there with you.'

'Ah!' he smiled tauntingly, as if something had at last given him satisfaction, 'Why not give him a ring, Neale? Say you've changed your mind and lunch with me?'

'No,' then hastily, as she found herself hesitating, 'I'd rather not.'

'Wouldn't you?' the sudden eagerness in his eyes turned to anger. 'For stubbornness, Neale, you take a lot of beating. You would rather be with me, a man who could teach you what life is all about, yet you won't give in. Why don't you stop nurturing all those crazy little inhibitions and learn to behave naturally?'

Neale felt her defences respond, freezing automatically. Glaring at him indignantly, she exclaimed. 'I don't want to go out with you, or to know you better!'

'Don't you?' he muttered belligerently, suddenly drawing her closer, dropping a brutal kiss on her open mouth before she could even guess at his intentions. A rippling shudder ran right through her body as the fierce pressure of his lips turned her blood to flames. He set her alight until she believed she was in danger of being totally consumed, and when he moulded her to him, his caressing hands sent shivers of desire dancing all over her skin, Neale trembled as his lips burned a path to her throat and beneath his exploring tongue her heart raced as she became entirely alive to the sensuous persuasion of his touch. She couldn't think, couldn't move, was utterly incapable of resisting him.

Only when she was almost completely helpless, arching herself against him involuntarily, did he put her from him, smiling confidently down into her bemused face.

'Now how about making that phone call?' he

breathed. 'We can have lunch in my apartment and bother about the south coast job another day.'

'No!' she was in no state to really understand him, her mind was still too befuddled by his lovemaking, but catching the drift of his suggestions, she recoiled in fright. Frantically she wrenched away from the hand still on her arm, her eyes sparkling with anger. 'I'll see you later, Mr Baillie,' she gasped, 'I should have thought you'd be the last one to advocate spending the afternoon wasting the firm's time!'

It was frustrating, when she had turned down Lawton's dubious offer with contempt, that she found little pleasure in Tony's company. The only solace she derived was in discovering for certain he meant nothing to her, that any hold he'd had over her was gone for ever. If it didn't make her feel any better towards men in general, at least it stopped her longing for what might have been.

Because Tony hadn't booked a table at the Grosvenor and time was limited—for both of them, she discovered—they decided to have a quick snack at a cafe near where Neale worked. The cafe wasn't comfortable for it was crowded and Neale found herself comparing Neale's slight figure with Lawton's powerful one until she could have screamed. Tony talked of his growing prestige in his father-in-law's business and how he wasn't getting on with his wife. He hinted that he might be coming to London a lot in future and would appreciate having someone to go around with while he was here.

He didn't seem to understand when Neale turned down his offer, which she decided was as questionable as the one Lawton had made. He wanted to see her again but she said she was busy.

'I realise I treated you badly but I promise to make it up to you,' he frowned. He was older than Neale but he looked like a small boy not getting his own way.

'You're married now, Tony,' she said gently, not

having either the heart or interest to say exactly what she thought. 'What happened between us doesn't matter anymore.'

'You'll keep in touch though?' he pleaded.

'I'll give you a ring, perhaps,' was as far as she would go, and refused to make it a promise.

Back in Lawton's office, she was surprised to find it empty. As he had called mockingly after her to be back not a minute later than two, she asked his secretary how long he would be? On being told by the woman that she had no idea, Neale forced herself to sit down and wait.

It was well after three before he appeared, by which time Neale was stiff with resentment. Having to twiddle her thumbs for the best part of two hours hadn't improved her temper. If it hadn't been for the note on his desk, commanding her not to leave, she wouldn't have waited five minutes!

As he walked past her, he was so reeking of perfume that after the initial shock, her mouth curled in distaste. It was obvious he hadn't lunched alone!

'Ah, good afternoon, Miss Curtis,' he settled himself expansively, immune to her annihilating glare. 'Have I kept you waiting? I'm afraid I forgot all about you. I'm sorry.'

He might have tried to look it! Neale wondered acidly whom he had been with? She was certain the tiny trace of lipstick on his mouth wasn't her colour!

'How was Tony?' he asked idly.

She swallowed. 'I'd be grateful if we could get on, Mr Baillie.'

'Your hair's coming loose,' he noted. 'It's beginning to escape down your neck. Have you checked the pins recently?'

'Please!' she breathed.

'Always impatient, aren't you?' his eyes strayed to her breasts where, to her horror, her nipples seemed to tauten to his considering gaze. 'In the right place it could be very exciting.'

If he hinted at that side of her nature once more she would scream. She was just about at boiling point anyway! 'Mr Baillie,' controlling her anger she tried again, 'I have a lot to do!'

'And to learn,' he growled, reaching for the phone, 'I have a call to make,' he barked to his secretary to get him a number. 'While I'm busy you can begin arranging your little bits and pieces on my desk—if you can find a space, as long as you don't move anything.'

She began with bad grace, her small face set mutinously as his call was prolonged and obviously not about business. When he finished, ignoring Neale, he buzzed for his secretary and started dictating complicated notes on a new deal he was negotiating somewhere in the Caribbean.

This concluded, he turned his attention to Neale but only until he remembered another call that couldn't wait and which kept him occupied for another considerable period.

Returning to the studios at six, Neale was so tense with frustration that she was sure she was in danger of bursting a blood vessel. Nothing had been accomplished, Lawton had merely glanced at what she was doing and kept her hanging about. When he had dismissed her he had said coolly that she had given him a lot to think about. He had smiled and she had wanted to hit him.

During the following days he kept her running between his office and the studios until she sometimes felt dizzy. He tormented her by insisting occasionally on changes she didn't want to make and didn't appear to understand, for all his professed knowledge of art, that it wasn't always possible to change one colour in a room without changing the lot!

'I'll be glad when Rex returns!' she was driven to muttering to Mildred darkly, but when Rex did return Lawton mysteriously disappeared. No one seemed to know where he was though all sorts of rumours flew round. Neale didn't mind that he had gone. Although he had made no attempt to touch her since the day she had refused his invitation to lunch, she had grown tired of having his taunting eyes roaming over her and having to constantly fight the wayward inclinations of her own treacherous heart.

If Rex regretted Lawton was gone, it was because within a few days, he and Neale had the south coast plans completed, ready for Lawton's final approval. And Lawton had left word that nothing was to go further than the planning stage without his personal verification. This caused Rex to fume, for he wanted the job finished so he could get on with the one in Spain, which definitely appeared to have captured his imagination.

'I shouldn't mind a week or two in Spain, myself,' Neale grumbled, one wet and windy morning as she reached the office positively dripping. 'What weather!'

'It won't be much better in Spain, just now,' Mildred pointed out prosaically.

'But the chances of it being better must be greater,' Neale retorted, struggling out of her mac.

'When you two girls have finished gossiping, I want to see you, Neale,' came Rex's voice.

Neale followed him to the small office, where he sometimes retired when things got too much for him. 'Trouble?' she asked, 'or good news for a change?'

'A bit of both,' he sighed, 'depending which way one looks at it.'

She hadn't expected him to take her query seriously. It had been meant merely as a teasing remark because he looked fed up. He usually liked to see her before he saw the others in the department, each morning, to give out the work for the day. At his terse tones, her brows rose slightly. 'Have I been doing something I shouldn't?'

'No,' he relaxed with a grin. 'Sorry if I seem on edge but I've just had the boss on the phone.'

'Mr Baillie?'

'Don't look so apprehensive,' Rex quirked. 'The good news concerns you.'

Was that supposed to make her feel better? Neale's unaccountable nervousness increased. 'Would you mind explaining?'

Rex nodded, 'I'll try. Lawton's in the Caribbean and he wants to see you immediately. I tried to tell him I couldn't do without you but it was a waste of breath.'

Neale was stunned. 'What does he want to see me about?'

'God give me strength!' Rex cried, tearing at his sparse hair. 'It's not you, he wants to see, it's the plans. You're to fly out with them, so we can make a start.'

How could she? Shock raced through her while every nerve in her body tightened in alarm. 'I can't go to the Caribbean, Rex. Didn't he mean you? You must have picked him up wrong!'

'I spoke to him myself, Neale,' Rex said shortly, 'I'm not that dense. There are two reasons why I'm not going. First, I wasn't asked. Second, Meg wouldn't be pleased, not after I've just got back from Spain. Anyway, Lawton considers it more important that I should be here, and I must agree he's right. All he wants is a look at what we've done. He doesn't think it likely that he will be changing anything but he wants to be sure.'

'I'll never wish for a few weeks in the sunshine again!' Neale groaned, but merely shook her head when Rex asked what she meant. She felt like a creature in a jungle sensing a trap but not sure where it was.

'Whereabouts is he in the Caribbean?' she recalled a telephone call Lawton had made when she had been in his office. That had been about the Caribbean, surely?

'You're to go to St Lucia.'

'Do you know if he's staying with friends or in a hotel?'

For a moment Rex looked almost envious. 'He's on his yacht.'

'Yacht?'

Rex grinned. 'That's startled you, has it?'

'Well, we can't all afford such trifling little toys.'

'Come on now, Neale!' Rex scolded, 'This isn't like you. Lawton deals in property, chiefly hotels, which makes a yacht almost essential. It can be embarrassing to stay in a hotel, say on an island, when you're planning to build one, as effective opposition, next to it.'

'I suppose so,' Neale sighed, then quickly. 'Isn't there anyone else you could send though? As a favour,' she begged with a coaxing smile she might at any other time been ashamed of, 'I'm really not keen.'

Rex grinned again. 'When you smile at me like that, Neale, if I wasn't so fond of my wife I might be tempted to leave her. Always supposing you'd have me, of course,' he added hastily. 'But, seriously,' his grin faded, 'even if I wanted to send someone else, I couldn't. Lawton asked for you specially.'

Neale flew straight from Heathrow to St Lucia and was met at the airport by a private car. The flight had been a long one but she felt more nervous than tired. On another occasion she might have been excited for she had never visited the Caribbean before, but the thought of her coming interview with Lawton was tying her stomach in knots.

She was whisked quickly from the airport by a driver who was clearly familiar with the routine. Her eyes wandered dazedly over the green, tropical beauty of the island through which they were passing. The skies were blue, the air warm and the sea looked so inviting she had a sudden longing to be swimming in it, but all she could really think of was seeing Lawton again. She hoped he would be free to study the layouts she had brought with her immediately, then she could go straight home.

They swept into Castries, the capital, taking the road to the yacht basin. Neale hadn't known what to expect but Lawton's yacht was magnificent. Long and white, it was moored, alongside others, in the tranquil waters of a defunct volcano crater. The driver took her on board where the Captain escorted her to where Lawton was waiting to see her.

Neale's heart was beating so fast as Lawton called for her to come in that her hand trembled as she opened the door.

'Neale!' he was on his feet instantly, drawing her into the cabin and closing the door. 'How are you?' dropping his head, he kissed her lightly on the cheek.

Drawing a sharp breath, she managed a cool smile. 'No better for being dragged thousands of miles.'

He laughed with genuine enjoyment. 'Think of the rewards, days of warm sunshine, and you'll soon forget the fatigue.'

She looked at him with alarm. 'I don't expect to be here that long. Rex said you just wanted a quick look at the completed plans.'

'There's no hurry,' he said soothingly. 'Are you annoyed because I wasn't at the airport? I intended to be but I got held up with business. You know I use the yacht as an office, as much as anything else? Unfortunately I don't like having a secretary aboard so I have to do it all myself.'

'I'm not annoyed,' she replied stiffly. 'It's just that I'd rather get back to work.'

He smiled and she was suddenly aware that he was standing so near there was scarcely any space between them. She swallowed as she noticed he was wearing only brief shorts and a shirt, unbuttoned to the waist which revealed much of his tall, powerful body. Again her breath caught as she clearly discerned the throb of his heart under the hair-covered skin and recalled what it had felt like against her own.

'You'll return to work as soon as I allow it,' he said arrogantly, his eyes fixed so closely on the perfect oval of her face that the colour in her cheeks heightened.

'I'm sure you'll find everything I've brought

satisfactory,' she was determined to stick to business. 'Rex is sure you'll be pleased.'

'I might be,' he dismissed the topic with infuriating indifference. 'You look very young with your hair like that, Neale. I don't want to see it pinned up while you're here.'

It had grown so uncomfortable on the plane that she had secured it to her nape with a piece of ribbon, letting the heavy masses of it fall down her back. 'I'll see,' she said warily.

His eyes narrowed intently. 'What are you afraid of, Neale? Is it yourself?'

'Myself?'

'You know what I mean, don't pretend not to.' As she began to protest, his hand went to her waist and he drew her closer, very persuasively, 'Are you afraid those inhibitions of yours might melt in a warmer climate and you will let me make love to you?'

She tried to control the languor spreading through her as something inside her responded to the softness of his tones. 'No, of course not!' she denied angrily. 'London, the Caribbean, makes no difference to me.'

'Doesn't it?' he murmured gently.

'You may keep me here,' she fought on fiercely, 'but I won't be wasting my time. I'll find something to do.'

'Let me show you your cabin,' he said soothingly, sliding his arm round her shoulders as he turned her towards the door. 'I use this cabin as an office as it is next to the one where I sleep. I can work through the night without disturbing anyone, when there's nothing else to do.'

Neale's heart accelerated again and she was glad she didn't have to look at him. Her cabin was beautiful, with a wide, soft bed and thick carpets. She even had her own bathroom and there was a vase of the most wonderful red roses on her bedside locker. With her trained eye for colour, she assessed and appreciated, unable to suppress an exclamation of delight.

'Change and come on deck,' Lawton turned abruptly from her expressive face. 'Wear whatever you've brought to swim in. I've other guests whom I'm sure you'll enjoy meeting again.'

'Meeting again?' Neale's feathery brows flew upwards for she had thought that, apart from the crew, there was no one on the yacht but herself. 'Who?'

'My sister-in-law, for one.'

Suddenly she smiled with such obvious relief that Lawton's mouth quirked ironically. 'It flatters me that this should make you feel so much better,' he murmured, before he disappeared.

The feeling of relief was joined by excitement as Neale quickly retrieved a bikini from her bag and went to the bathroom. June being here did make her feel better. She refused to believe she was using June as an excuse for letting the high spirits which had been subdued for years, show through. If Lawton insisted she stayed, well, as he was the boss, there was nothing she could do about it. She may as well enjoy herself while she could!

As she changed, she was glad she had allowed Mildred to persuade her into buying a new bikini and matching cover-up. Mildred had made all the arrangements for her flight and had been full of advice. When Neale had insisted she would be coming straight back, she had said it wouldn't be possible, and she would have to spend at least two nights in a hotel. She had accompanied Neale on a shopping trip to Harrods and the blue, lilac and beige striped bikini looked gorgeous, if far too brief.

She skipped up on deck, subsiding to a more dignified pace as she neared the spot where she could hear people talking. There was a spacious sun-deck, half covered by awning, and she paused for a moment taking in the scene. Several comfortable chairs were scattered round a large area and June was lying on one, looking much fitter than she had when Neale had seen her in London.

Freddy, her husband, was there and, to Neale's surprise, the voluptuous redhead who had lost her earring in Lawton's London apartment. The stranger talking to him on the other side of the deck must be her husband. Unless she was here alone.

Unable to remain in hiding any longer, she went over to June and spoke to her. When June heard her voice, she looked up, her eyes warm and friendly. 'Oh, hello, Neale,' she smiled. 'It's lovely to see you again. Come and sit down. I don't think you've met Evonne and Brian?'

'Latimer,' Lawton helped with the introductions suavely, leaving the rail to make sure Neale was comfortable. 'What are you having to drink?'

'Nothing too strong after that flight,' she smiled ruefully. 'My tummy still doesn't feel it's on the ground.'

'Aren't you used to flying?' Evonne asked haughtily, letting her glance wander over Neale coolly, without turning her head.

'I'm a working girl,' Neale replied, trying not to be disconcerted by the woman's obvious disparagement, 'I rarely manage to get very far.'

'She is thinking of going further, in future,' Lawton murmered laconically, bringing Neale an innocently coloured concoction in a tall glass and letting his hand rest lightly on her shoulder.

She wished she could get out of the habit of reading different meanings into everything he said! She started as he gently removed her cover-up, leaving her exposed to the sun, and more curious glances. She felt suddenly too slender and too young and just too naive to cope with any of the people here. She could never hope to achieve their degree of sophistication. When June intervened to ask for details about her journey, she turned to her gratefully.

Lunch was served shortly afterwards by two of the sure-footed crew with which the yacht appeared to

abound. On low tables on the deck was laid a
wonderful buffet to which everyone helped themselves.
There were numerous crisp salads and cold meats as
well as delicious coquilles of fish, served in a tempting
wine sauce with mushrooms. To finish off there was
fruit salad and a bewildering selection of fresh fruit
followed by coffee and cheese.

Neale was hungry, having eaten little for the past two
days and practically nothing on the plane. She had been
so overwrought at the thought of having to come here
that it had completely ruined her appetite. Greedily she
gobbled down a large plateful, consisting of a bit of
almost everything and Lawton laughed.

'It's the first time I've known you eat a good meal.'

If he adds I look as though I could do with one, I'll
throw something! Neale lowered her eyes so he couldn't
read her mind but he merely smiled and suggested they
did a tour of the boat.

Neale was surprised how eager she was to see it.
Following him, she felt so light-hearted that when he
caught hold of her hand, she let it lie unprotesting in his
strong fingers. If his touch sent prisms of warmth
shooting through her, she was ready for the reaction
and managed to control it.

'Where shall we start first,' he murmured, 'my cabin?'
He relented when her cheeks went pink and she was
obviously nervous, 'All right, we can do the upper deck
first then see how we feel.'

The lounge was like a room in a large London
house, extremely elegant but comfortable. Neale was
amazed by its size and was similarly impressed by the
dining room. It was an equally spacious apartment,
complete with a long polished table and chairs. The
walls were fitted with units which she imagined held
china and cutlery along with other things. Through
the porthole, which more resembled a real window,
she saw the afternoon sun shimmering on the water
of the harbour and again, as had happened earlier,

she felt her pulses responding and quckening with excitement.

'It's all so entrancing!' she rounded on Lawton, her eyes wide and dazed. 'Don't you love it?'

His eyes were on her face. 'I'm trying not to but I think I'm fighting a losing battle.'

She frowned, for his meaning wasn't clear. 'If I were you, I don't think I could bear to leave it.'

'I do spend a lot of time on board,' he smiled, 'if not always here, in similar places. It makes a change to return to London. Then sometimes I get tired of travelling and long for a settled home.'

Her heart gave a strange little jump. 'Would that content you for long?'

'Probably not,' he shrugged.

He took her down the companion-way to the lower deck where her cabin was and proceeded to show her the others. His stateroom was near hers, on the other side of his office, but he did no more than open the door briefly.

'June looks well,' she said, as he indicated the quarters she shared with Freddy. 'She was telling me, at lunch, how much better she feels since coming to St Lucia.'

'She certainly needed a change,' he frowned, leaving Neale to wonder what to make of his sudden grimness. She hoped things weren't that bad between June and his brother. Was Lawton trying to heal the breach between them by bringing them together like this? Or was he attempting to prove that the breach was unbridgeable?

They toured on until Neale was nodding and answering sleepily and Lawton's eyes softened as they lingered on her tired face. Firmly he retraced their steps to her own cabin, ushering her in and closing the door.

'To bed with you, for an hour or two.' He gave her a little push towards it as she began to protest. 'I'll wait until you're under the sheets, then I'll be certain you're obeying orders.'

She wasn't going to get into bed with him there! Her pulses were throbbing too wildly as it was, through spending the past hours with him, without putting further strain on them.

'I can manage,' she said quickly.

'Take something light to the bathroom and get out of your bikini, you'll be more comfortable.'

Throwing an incensed glance, which he ignored as easily as the remark she had made, she delved in her bag again. She felt driven to find an excuse for the thinness of the silky wrapper she drew out. 'I wasn't able to bring a lot. Anyway, I didn't think I'd be staying.'

'Run along,' he said coolly, 'I'll unpack the rest for you, while you're busy.'

'I can do that later,' she snapped.

'Neale!' he barked. And she fled.

CHAPTER FIVE

WHEN she returned, wearing the clinging robe through which she was certain Lawton could see every curve of her figure, her bags had disappeared and he was closing the closet door. The gleam of satisfaction in his eyes brought a flicker of alarm to Neale's as she realised he had done what he'd said he would do.

'You've been careful with the files, I hope?'

'I've put them in my office,' he assured her. 'You're welcome to go there any time and I thought it would be the best place to go over them together. Eventually.'

'Oh, well, thank you,' while his softening expression forgave her for suspecting him of carelessness, she shuffled with embarrassment, bowing her head.

'Into bed with you,' he moved so silently she didn't hear him draw nearer and glanced up, startled, as he grasped the edge of the sheet and manoeuvred her under it. 'What you need is a nursemaid, my girl.'

The sheets were blissfully cool, if only the temperature of her blood would drop accordingly. Doubtfully, she looked at Lawton through her long lashes. 'Somehow I can't see you in such a role!'

'You'd be surprised,' he replied solemnly. 'Do you know I've always hankered after a job like that. I'm very good at taking things off and tucking in.'

'I bet!' she retorted fiercely, suddenly angry as she envisaged the number of women he must have helped in this way. His affairs were not exactly a secret!

'Do I detect a note of jealousy?'

His mouth was twitching. He couldn't possibly be laughing at her? 'Of course not!' she exclaimed, wondering how she might convince him that the anger in her voice had been mockery.

Apparently she failed, for he smiled broadly. 'You can leave me now,' she said primly.

He growled, deep in his throat. 'Proper little madam, aren't you, ordering me about?'

Flushing with mortification, she knew he was right. She shouldn't forget she was merely a lowly employee. He was tolerant, just as long as she didn't try and upstage him. 'I'm sorry,' she whispered, 'I wasn't thinking.'

'People who say one thing while they're thinking another are usually confused.' Sitting on the bed, he bent over her sardonically, one hand lifting to her face then sliding to her nape to remove the ribbon from her hair. While her limbs were incapable of movement, he slowly spread some thick, gleaming strands across her pillows. 'Didn't you once tell me it was a sight I would never see?' he murmured.

Neale drew a quick breath, her lips parting, as his eyes glowed triumphantly. How could she keep cool when he taunted her so devastatingly? She was as helpless as a rabbit and he knew it. One false move might bring her straight into his arms and this was something she couldn't risk. Silently she glared at him, declining to answer.

His low laughter was again full of mockery. 'You have to look furious, I suppose. It's all part of this ridiculous defensive attitude, I assume.' Taking another handful of hair, he trailed it down her throat, watching its pale colour glitter against her breast. Then gently he lowered his head and kissed her.

'I'm going now,' he said softly, the touch of his lips featherlight. 'But I might not always be so easily dismissed. Just keep that in mind.'

When he had gone, she was sure she wouldn't sleep but she did. The kiss he had left on her mouth had contained no pressure but her lips tingled as though they had been crushed. And her whole body trembled and seemed on fire, a feeling she had never experienced with Tony. She couldn't understand how a man she had been engaged to had failed to stir her in a similar fashion.

She tried to convince herself, as she had done several time before, that she didn't even like Lawton Baillie, but she knew she was merely attempting to paste over the cracks in her defences. She didn't want to fall in love, if this was what was happening to her, but it seemed love didn't care whether it was welcome or not. It arrived, barged in, took over and the best one might do was pretend it wasn't there. Comparing what she had felt for Tony with her feelings for Lawton was like comparing diluted beer with the strongest spirits. There was just no comparison but she mustn't let Lawton destroy her. He enjoyed the fun of the chase, as was evident from the odd snippets of gossip her memory was producing. Hadn't he pursued other women—almost making headlines—then dropped them after short periods? Which was what he would do with Neale Curtis, if once she gave in to him. With a warning so clear it might have been printed in large letters before her very eyes, wouldn't she be a fool if she took no notice?

It was after seven when she awoke to find Lawton standing over her. He had an absorbed but unreadable expression on his face and she wondered how long he had been there.

'You should have called me earlier,' she gasped, dismayed at the time.

'You brought a dress,' he said, 'I hung it in your wardrobe. I'll give you exactly fifteen minutes to get into it.'

Was he always to be ordering her about! 'I had expected to be spending the night in a hotel.' She proffered the excuse for packing her new white chiffon wondering uneasily if it was the right one?

'We're dining in one of the island hotels,' he was already striding out. 'The others have gone on ahead, so get a move on.'

He really was the limit, she grumbled to herself, but exactly fifteen minutes later she met him on deck. 'I've had a terrible rush!' she complained, determined not to notice how attractive he looked in his formal evening wear. 'I feel only half dressed.'

Lawton smiled. 'If you're fishing for compliments you don't need to, you always look beautiful.' His eyes darkened as they lingered on her slender figure. 'You have such good taste that a man might be willing to spend a fortune on you. I'd like to buy you all sorts of things, including furs and jewellery.'

When she froze, he rebuked her softly. 'Don't let's have an argument about the inevitable right now. I promised to go to this party and I'd rather not be the last to arrive. As it is we're going to be late.'

'Do I have to go?' she was stiff with resentment at the things he had been saying.

'Yes!' he replied, adamantly.

Silently she walked down the gangway with him to the waiting car. He was driving himself. As he started off she asked curiously. 'Do you always stay in the harbour?'

'No,' he was giving most of his attention to getting through the capital. 'It's convenient when I'm doing business but usually I hate staying in the one place for long. Today I waited for you.'

Neale had read and heard that St Lucia was one of the loveliest islands in the Southern Caribbean but she had never been able to afford to come and see for herself. Since starting work she had saved most of her money towards renting and furnishing a flat. Once she had managed to find one it seemed to take all her spare cash. Next year she had thought she might manage Spain. She had never expected to be here today.

The colours were vivid, appealing to her artistic eye though some of them were so bright she couldn't envisage them in England. As they left Castries and travelled north, the road was as good as it was scenic.

Noting the pale, cresent-shaped beaches, idly lapped by blue seas and white-crested waves, her eyes began sparkling with interest.

'It all looks so lovely!' she cried, not ashamed of sounding naive, 'Everything looks so alive, Lawton!'

'I'll show you it all before we go home,' he glanced at her intently. 'That's a promise.'

Her face sparkled with pleasure and her fervent 'Thank you,' was rewarded with an answering smile.

He told her that many of the island's best hotels were situated in the north, and, as they approached a number of them, she asked, 'Is the land you're negotiating for round here?'

'Yes,' he replied, without being more explicit.

She frowned as they pulled under a colourful awning and the car stopped. 'Have you had trouble?'

'Not what you'd call trouble,' as he helped her out, the light breeze caught her hair and he flicked a strand back in place. 'I hope to have everything completed in another day or two.'

The hotel loomed above them, it's balconies ablaze with flowers as were the grounds. The actual building appeared to go on and on. It was painted white with all the sophisticated trappings that usually embellished such establishments and looked very attractive.

The others were waiting for them. 'We'd nearly given you up!' June cried.

'It's my fault,' Neale confessed, shame-facedly, 'I overslept.'

'Jet lag,' Lawton kept an arm around her as he ushered her inside. 'It affected her badly. I had to wake her up.'

Did he have to tell them that! Neale saw the raised eyebrows and flushed. 'It won't happen again,' she said then wished she'd kept quiet as Freddy grinned sceptically, causing, she realised bitterly, her relationship with Lawton to be exposed to even greater speculation!

There was quite a party. Lawton's friend was

departing after a lengthy stay and half the island seemed to have gathered to wish him farewell. Dinner was a noisy but pleasant affair and afterwards there was dancing.

'There's dancing every night,' June laughed. 'Sometimes I think it's all people do round here.'

'I'm not complaining,' Freddy's eyes were trained on a luscious blonde but so far he was only looking. Lawton glanced at him cynically while June's laughter wobbled slightly and she sighed. Evonne was dancing with her husband and looked bored.

Someone hailed Lawton from the other side of the room and while he was gone a young man, whom she had sensed was watching her, asked Neale to dance. She was about to refuse when she decided he looked harmless enough and changed her mind.

It was unpleasant to discover, a few minutes later, that she had made a mistake. Her partner obviously believed that dancing with a girl gave him licence to do as he liked. He began holding her too closely and when she protested he steered her out on the terrace which ran alongside the ballroom.

'The moon is too good to waste,' he told a startled Neale, laughing as he swung her expertly into a shadowy corner, away from the inside lights.

'Will you please let me go?' Neale exclaimed between her teeth as his hands began wandering intimately over her, arousing nothing but disgust.

'Shut up, honey,' he complained. 'I don't find a girl like you every day. You're far too gorgeous to be mean. How about a few kisses?' he suggested, nuzzling wet lips against her cheek.

'No!' Neale choked, attempting to push him away, even as Lawton snapped coldly, 'What the hell do you think you're doing with my partner, Lewin?'

With a smothered curse, Lewin released her. Neale was no less surprised to see Lawton than he was and listened numbly as he stuttered an apology on whisky-laden breath.

'Are you all right?' Lawton asked grimly, as Neale's would-be abductor disappeared.

Now that she was safe, Neale's fear disappeared too. It was replaced by resentment which, oddly enough, seemed directed at Lawton rather than the man who had just left them. Instead of thanking Lawton for rescuing her, she found herself saying coldly, 'You don't have to follow me round like a watch-dog, you know. I can look after myself.

'A fine job you were making of it,' he jeered.

'I'm sure—Mr Lewin, didn't you call him? didn't mean to make a nuisance of himself.'

Lawton glared at her and said bluntly. 'Not many women who know him would share your views. He's only just bearable when he's sober.'

'I still wish you wouldn't interfere!' she retorted sharply, thinking obscurely, her only hope lay in keeping Lawton at a distance. Already she had forgotten the other man and was trying to control an impulse to throw herself into Lawton's arms. A gleam of moonlight struck his strong, chiselled features, playing havoc with her emotions, making her heart race.

'You call saving you from that scoundrel interfering?' Lawton asked, his voice degrees colder.

'Yes!' lifting her chin, she challenged him to deny it.

'Very well,' his eyes narrowed to chilling slits. 'My apologies, Miss Curtis, if I blundered. I promise not to make the same mistake again, but it will be interesting to see how you get on without me.'

His face set and hard, he turned away, leaving her to follow. Neale gazed after him, regret flooding over her. She felt both guilty and ungrateful and found no relief in the knowledge that she had probably alienated him completely. Swallowing down a lump in her throat, she trailed unhappily back to the ballroom.

The party was in full swing with drinks flowing steadily. Unnoticed, she stood on her own for several minutes before Evonne and Freddy found her.

'We're thinking of visiting a nightclub further along the coast,' Freddy grinned. 'How about coming with us, as a chaperon?'

'Chaperon?'

At Neale's confused expression, Freddy's innocent grin broadened. Grabbing her arm, he gave it a confiding squeeze. 'Both our spouses are inclined to be jealous, as you've probably already perceived. But they won't be able to complain if you're with us.'

'Please!' Evonne added her persuasions. She even managed to smile at Neale, something she hadn't done until now.

Feeling a flicker of distaste, Neale was about to refuse when she happened to catch sight of Lawton dancing with a sultry looking female with an even more voluptuous figure than Evonne's. She was draped all over him, her arms round his neck and he appeared to be whispering in her ear. At his apparent enjoyment, Neale felt a sword twisting in her heart.

'You don't have to worry about Lawton,' Freddy said slyly, following the direction of her glance. 'If I know Lydia, he's going to be occupied for the rest of the night. They're old friends.'

This decided Neale. She couldn't bear to wait and see whether Freddy was speaking the truth. She feared the suspense might kill her. Tearing her eyes from the depressing sight of Lawton making love to the other girl, she followed Evonne and Freddy from the room.

The nightclub was practically next door. When Neale discovered this she was peculiarly relieved, but her relief became tinged with apprehension again as she realised it wasn't the smoochy cabaret in the restaurant that was the attraction for her two companions, but the gaming tables in a room in the basement.

'Don't you play?' Freddy asked, as Evonne slipped into a vacant chair at one of the tables and patted the seat next to her impatiently. As Neale shook her head, he encouraged, 'Well, now's your chance. Why not have a go?'

'I'd really prefer to watch,' she replied.

To give Freddy his due, he didn't try to over persuade her. He merely shrugged, his eye already on the croupier. 'Just stick by me,' he advised, 'and you won't come to any harm.'

Freddy's advice might have been well meant but it wasn't easy to follow. As the crush of onlookers grew, Neale was constantly pushed and squashed until she felt bruised. It soon became impossible to find a comfortable spot from which to view the game and when someone stood heavily on her toes, she retreated.

As she wriggled her toes experimentally, hoping there was no permanent damage, a man spoke to her. He was middle-aged and had a charming smile which she found soothing.

'Aren't you with Mr Fielding?' he asked.

'Yes and no,' she smiled, liking the man immediately, 'I came with Mr Fielding and a friend. I don't play but I was trying to watch,' she added ruefully.

The man nodded sympathetically. 'There's usually a crowd. Are you on holiday?'

Neale shook her head wryly, 'I suppose I could say I was on a working holiday but that's all.'

His eyes lit with interest. 'My dear, you must let me buy you a drink while you tell me why a beautiful young girl like yourself should have to work for a living?'

'I'd rather not, thank you.' Neale found nothing offensive in what seemed a kindly suggestion but she was more interested in returning to the yacht. 'I'll just wait for my friends.'

He laid a hand on her arm. 'Once Freddy starts playing he doesn't know when to stop. If you don't want a drink, how about coffee? It's not so hot upstairs and it won't take long.'

Because he apparently knew Freddy well and Freddy had obviously forgotten her existence, she gave in. If

she went with this nice man he might be able to tell her
how to get back to the yacht. She had no intention of
returning to the other hotel and seeking help from
Lawton!

Still holding her arm, the man guided her from the
casino. At the bottom of the stairs he turned right.

'This isn't the way, surely?' Neale frowned.

'A short cut,' he smiled.

'No,' after a few yards, she held back intuitively
uneasy, 'I've changed my mind.'

As she tried to release her arm, which she hadn't
realised he was holding so tightly, he pulled her into his
arms before she could escape.

'I wasn't wrong about you, darling. I couldn't be!
You smiled at me and needed little persuasion to leave
your friends. It's too late to change your mind.'

Horrified. Neale stared at him, wondering just what
she had got herself into? Lawton's words returned to
taunt her. If only she had listened to him! 'How could I
be attracted to you?' she gasped, 'when I've only known
you five minutes.'

He smiled, a leering smile, that altered his benign
appearance amazingly. 'Come on now, honey, don't
split hairs. You must know what I'm talking about.'

'I don't!' she cried, but it was too late. With a strength
that surprised her, he began dragging her along.

'We'll go to my place,' he muttered, licking his loose
lips. 'You have nothing to lose by being nice to me, I
promise.'

'No!' she reiterated, disbelieving it was possible for a
girl to get in the same fix twice on the same evening!
Where was he taking her to? Terror motivated her to
dig her heels in but there wasn't much to get them into.
The smooth carpet under her feet was like glass. Feeling
herself sliding, she hit out at him wildly but he only
laughed.

As the horrible sound of his laughter flowed over her,
she shuddered. This man made the man Lewin's

advances seem innocent by comparison, and, with a sob in her throat she doubted if there would be anyone to help her this time. Everyone seemed to be upstairs or in the casino. The corridor was deserted.

Then, as she flung back her head and made another attempt to free herself, her eyes widened as they met a pair of furious blue ones. In another moment she was released as Lawton flung her assailant aside with a force that must have jarred every bone in his body. He slid to the floor looking very frightened, throwing up instinctive hands to protect himself, as if he expected to be flattened.

'I didn't mean anything,' he muttered, visibly shrivelling as Lawton glared at him. 'I didn't know, sir, that this was your young lady.'

'Whose young lady she is shouldn't have anything to do with it,' Lawton snapped coldly, his clenched fists more than hinting at the inclinations he was just managing to control. 'Men like you ought to be locked up. I'll personally be doing my best to make sure you don't get a chance to assault anyone else.'

'I'm sorry,' the man whined sullenly.

Neale tried to speak but before she could find her voice, Lawton was bundling her savagely back upstairs and out of the building. 'My wrist!' she gasped hoarsely.

'Just be grateful it isn't your neck!'

'I realise I shouldn't have come here,' she whispered incoherently, still shaking from her ordeal.

His hold on her wrist tightened punishingly. She could feel his anger stabbing her through his fingertips. 'Your foolishness won't go unrewarded!' he grated. 'And when I catch up with my brother he will wish he had never been born!'

Neale trembled with fright as Lawton hauled her brutally to his car. 'Freddy was only trying to help,' she had some vague notion of defending him. 'You were too busy to look after me.'

At the accusation in her voice, Lawton's lips quirked slightly and a little of the anger died from his face. His eyes were still cold though, as he taunted, 'You said you could do without my help, remember?'

'Yes,' she sighed, 'I know I did. I have to be independent. Anyway,' she added unwisely, 'You didn't have to leave your girl-friend to come after me.'

'Believe me,' he looked incensed, 'if I didn't consider you my responsibility, I wouldn't have!'

'I'm sorry,' she murmured tearfully, all the fight suddenly going out of her, 'I shouldn't have said that. I don't know what would have happened if you hadn't turned up. That man was horrible.'

Ignoring her tears, Lawton switched on the ignition and roared back to the harbour. On board again, he took her to his office where he poured two drinks. Thrusting one into her hands, he said curtly.

'For a girl as intelligent as you are, Neale, your naivety never ceases to amaze me. That place you've been in this evening isn't designed for girls wandering about on their own. Men like the one you were involved with abound, and it's difficult to pin anything on to them when their victims rarely complain. Few are so innocent, anyway, that the men who pick them up could be accused of rape.'

Neale felt herself growing colder. 'I thought we were just going to have a cup of coffee.'

The blue eyes changed to steel. 'You must have known the risk you were taking, accepting any kind of invitation from the likes of him.'

'He seemed harmless enough,' Neale faltered, her whole body freezing when she realised the escape she had had.

Lawton didn't spare her, despite her white face. 'You're far too trusting. You might have been scarred for life, the marks your fiancé left, nothing by comparison.'

Neale's gulped, her distress suddenly very evident. 'I

really am grateful that you rescued me, Lawton. I didn't know what I was going to do.'

His mouth tightened, a pulse pounding in the hardness of his jaw. 'I'll murder Freddy!'

Neale thought of Evonne. 'Evonne's there, too,' she whispered unhappily, 'won't her husband be worrying?'

'Evonne,' Lawton said cynically, 'can look after herself. If she can't find a man willing to entertain her, she turns to gambling.'

Briefly diverted by the dryness of his tone, Neale asked impulsively, 'If you don't like Evonne, why are she and her husband here?'

Lawton looked at her grimly. 'Brian works for me. I had to have him for this deal being negotiated and he asked if he could bring his wife along.'

'I see,' Neale raised her tired head and began thanking Lawton again for what he had done for her. But he merely lifted a halting hand, dismissing her faltering words brusquely.

'Go to bed, Neale,' he said. 'I'll see you tomorrow. It will be thanks enough if you remember what I've said and try to grow up.'

She went to sleep, disturbed and unhappy and woke feeling the same way. Dressing quickly she went up on deck, hoping to find Lawton, but there was no one about. He wasn't having breakfast, either, and though Neale drank some coffee, she couldn't face anything else. Her appetite was as depressed as her spirits. Lawton must still be angry with her and the thought did nothing to cheer her up.

By making discreet enquiries, she learned that he and Brian had gone ashore. Having decided he was deliberately avoiding her, to learn he wasn't was a relief, but it could be hours before he returned and she knew if she was forgiven.

As lunch wasn't usually until two o'clock, she spent the hours between pacing restlessly. The view from the yacht, entrancing at first, soon lost its appeal, as did the

activities of the sailors swabbing the decks. Feeling full
of frustrated energy, she felt like offering to give them a
hand but if she did she feared they would be
embarrassed. By the time Lawton came back her soft
mouth was drooping unconsciously.

She was watching the road to the yacht basin when
Lawton's car swept along it, but he scarcely glanced at
her as he came aboard. Brian spoke but he merely
nodded, and, because his offhand treatment of her hurt,
she clenched her hands in silent despair against the way
her heart reacted to the sight of his tall, lean figure. He
was wearing a short-sleeved white shirt and white
trousers and each time she saw him he seemed to be
taller and broader, a fact that did nothing to steady her
racing pulse.

She heard him giving an order to one of the stewards
before he disappeared below. Impulsively she almost
followed him but rather than risk another snub she
forced herself to remain where she was.

When lunch was served he joined them, and if he
didn't exactly ignore Neale, he talked mostly with the
others. Freddy's absence was noted and remarked on.
June explained he was still asleep and Evonne said
carelessly that it was no wonder, considering the
amount he had imbibed the night before, but Neale
wondered if he wasn't expediently keeping out of the
way in the hope that Lawton might forget what had
happened at the casino? June had asked her earlier how
she had got home and although she had glossed over
most of it, June had looked alarmed and hurried off
again, no doubt to warn Freddy.

They ate on deck and, afterwards, Lawton wandered
with his coffee to the rails. Taking a deep breath, Neale
went after him, but when she suggested they looked over
the completed portfolio for the hotel, he shrugged
coldly.

'I'm tied up for the rest of the afternoon, Neale.
Perhaps tomorrow?'

Always tomorrow! She watched him despondently as he drained his cup and turned away. She found it difficult to acknowledge that his refusal to check her work didn't bother her half as much as the coolness of his present attitude. Neale shivered slightly, though the sun was hot, before a kind of paralysis gripped her as she began wondering what was happening to her?

They stayed on board that evening. June and Evonne had slept until noon but declared they were still tired. Neale wasn't tired so much as restless, but having no wish for a repetition of the previous evening, she was quite happy to stay on the yacht. She recognised the restlessness inside her for what it was, a suddenly feverish desire for something she had never had, something which, since Tony, she hadn't allowed herself to even think about. Until meeting Lawton Baillie!

When June and Freddy joined the other couple for bridge, after dinner, Neale pleaded she would like an early night. There seemed no point in sitting around and the moonlight on deck had to be shared with someone. Lawton surprised her by following her below. As she opened her cabin door she was startled to hear him abruptly call her name.

'Neale!' swiftly he caught up with her, turning her round, his voice softening, 'How have you been?'

With his eyes intently searching her pale face, Neale was so confused, she wasn't sure.

'None the better for having you cross with me,' she confessed weakly, unable to hide her unhappiness.

A brow rose quizzically. 'Where did you get that impression?'

A small sigh of exasperation escaped Neale. 'You can't pretend you haven't been. You haven't spoken to me all day!'

'Haven't I?' Tiny flickers of light danced in his eyes at the reproach in her voice. 'I distinctly remember speaking to you after lunch.'

She dropped her head, feeling choked. 'You don't call that. . . .'

'Hush!' gently, his hand curving her chin, he used his thumb to close her indignant lips. When he made her look at him, she blinked to see his usually steely blue eyes warm with amusement. 'I've been busy today, Neale. Getting this deal tied up hasn't been easy. I may have to return to London for consultations but I hope not immediately. I'll admit I was angry last night, and I think I had reason, but I don't bear grudges.'

'Don't you?' she murmured doubtfully, grey eyes bright.

'You have to allow me some leeway,' he grinned. 'Sometimes you act like a wilful child, and the only way I want to deal with you, you refuse.'

The colour flew to Neale's cheeks as his eyes fell deliberately on the fulness of her breasts curving seductively above her narrow waist. 'That man didn't harm you, did he?' he asked huskily.

'No.'

'Am I forgiven then?' he murmured softly, leaning nearer so she could feel his cool breath on her face.

'I think that question really belongs to me,' she replied, with a tentative smile.

'Let's agree there were faults on both sides then?' he teased, trailing his hands down her bare arms before lifting them to clasp his neck as he drew her closer. 'Shall we kiss and make up?' he suggested mischievously.

Neale gazed at him, her lips trembling until he bent his head and took possession of them, by which time her eyes had closed helplessly. Like the other occasions when he had kissed her, the sensation created in them both was like a powerful drug, rendering them unconscious to everything except each other. Lawton's hands on her back slid to her hips, pressing her tightly to the hardness of his body. Exquisite pain flooded Neale's being, the pain of consuming desire and unsatisfied needs.

With a small groan of surrender, her hands came round to caress his face before her fingers threaded with remembered pleasure through the thick softness of his hair. She pressed even closer as Lawton's mouth parted hers with insistent, demanding pressure.

Another moment and he drew back, his eyes smouldering, his breathing heavy. 'Will you let me make love to you, Neale?' he asked thickly.

'Tonight?' she whispered.

'Tomorrow,' he said, putting her firmly from him. 'Tomorrow we will spend the whole day together. I know an island where we can be completely alone. Will you come?' When she nodded dazedly, he gave a groan of satisfaction and added, 'Be ready at eleven, darling, meet me on deck.'

Although the commitment she had made frightened her, causing her to lose sleep, Neale was ready at the appointed time. During the morning had come an increasing certainty that Lawton had no serious intentions of seducing her. Last night, like herself, he had got a little carried away. Now that he'd had time to think things over, she had doubts that he would even wish to spend the day with her but she couldn't resist the temptation to go and see.

She was comfortable in a pair of white shorts, which June had found for her yesterday, and thin white top. She wore her bikini underneath, so that if Lawton should change his mind, he needn't know about it. He hadn't changed his mind, though, and a sense of the inevitable struck her sharply as she saw him waiting to help her down into a white launch.

As they skimmed over the water, away from the yacht and out of the harbour, she was still trying to find all the logical excuses she'd thought of to avoid going with him. When she had seen him standing against the rail, something in his eyes as he'd watched her approach had sent everything else out of her mind. Now she gave up. Was there any sense in fighting a battle already half lost? Shaking her blonde head, so that her hair whipped like silver in the wind, she decided to stop worrying and let the day take care of itself.

'I didn't know you could sail,' she said, as Lawton turned along the coast then began putting a greater distance between themselves and land.

His mouth smiled but his eyes were more serious. 'You don't know much about me, do you?'

'Not really,' she reflected slowly, glancing away from him warily.

'Don't worry,' he laughed, making for the open sea. 'There's a lot I don't know about you. We can always swop information.'

Immediately Neale tensed. There was a lot he would never know, neither he nor anyone else! There was so much locked deep inside her she could never bear to speak of. The freezing process continued but she was suddenly grateful for its cooling affect. It enabled her to pretend she was totally indifferent to the superbly constructed masculine figure seated so close to her. It helped her to forget a promise she had made in a moment of madness—a madness which she was sure, if encouraged to run its course, would only mean disaster for both of them!

CHAPTER SIX

THINKING it might be better to change the subject, Neale asked stiffly. 'Won't the others be feeling neglected?'

'Why should they?' he countered lightly. 'Brian and Evonne are visiting old friends on St Lucia and June and Freddy, when I asked them, said they were going to laze on the yacht.'

Did that mean he had invited them? Neale would liked to have known but murmured instead, 'I hope you weren't angry with Freddy for taking me to the casino?'

Lawton's mouth quirked at her visible apprehension. 'There were certain things that needed saying, but, don't worry, Freddy thrives on little lectures.'

She retorted tartly, 'I suspect that scarcely describes one of yours!'

'He always comes back for more,' Lawton shrugged, 'which must prove something.'

'That they have no effect?'

Lawton's brows rose. 'I hate to imagine what would happen if I didn't bother to check him occasionally, but if you believe I enjoy doing it you're wrong. Over the years it has grown tedious.'

Neale grimaced. 'I suppose, like me, you're waiting for him to grow up?'

'Did I say that?'

'Yes,' she replied, unable to hide her resentment.

He appraised her thoughtfully. 'You look about fifteen in that outfit. So young and innocent, I find it difficult to remember you're a woman.'

The way he said woman brought a shiver of doubt to Neale's eyes. Lawton had decided she was experienced. If he ever discovered she wasn't he would feel deceived.

Once, at a party, she had overheard a man remarking that inexperienced girls were more of a liability than anything else. 'My shorts belong to June,' she said hastily, pretending to misunderstand him. 'They're an old pair she used to wear before she was-er-expecting the baby.'

'You can't be trying to spare my blushes?' Lawton eyed her mockingly, 'I do know where babies come from.'

Neale nodded stoically, hating him for making her feel foolishly embarrassed. Abruptly she turned from his amused glance, forcing her attention elsewhere. The sea glittered, a hundred shades of blue, and she gazed in amazement at the shoals of brightly coloured fish swimming in the crystal-clear water. She was so intrigued she might have fallen overboard, but for Lawton's warning.

'I've never seen anything like it!' she cried excitedly. 'Why don't you take a look?'

'I'd rather look at you,' he said softly, watching enthusiasm making her face glow. 'Fish aren't nearly as enchanting, but if you like I can pretend you're a mermaid?'

'I don't happen to have a tail,' she retorted carelessly, too bewitched by the marine life around them to take much notice of what he was saying.

'Just as well,' he teased, 'a tail wouldn't be nearly as accommodating.'

Something in his voice made her pulse race and she was so busy trying to steady it, she failed to see immediately when the smooth surface of the ocean was suddenly broken by a pile of white surf. 'What on earth is that?' she exclaimed in surprise, when she did.

'Are you scared?' Lawton asked, and when she shook her head, having complete trust in his navigational skills, he explained, 'It's a coral reef. Many of the islands are ringed by them and the sea batters against them, thus saving the island from it's full force. On the

YOURS FREE

4 Harlequin Presents® *and a fashion tote*

It's our way of introducing you to our Harlequin Reader Service that's so much easier and less expensive than buying your novels retail.

As a subscriber, you'll receive 6 new books to preview every month. Always before they're available in stores. Always for the same low price. Always with the right to return the shipment and owe nothing.

P2TMU

►► FREE BOOKS & TOTE BAG ◄◄

YES, please send me 4 **FREE** Harlequin Presents and my **FREE** tote bag. Then send me 6 new Harlequin Presents each month. Bill me for only $1.75 each (for a total of $10.50 per shipment—a saving of $1.20 off retail price). There are no shipping, handling or other hidden charges. I can cancel anytime. The 4 free novels and tote bag are mine to keep, even if I never buy a book from Harlequin.

106 CIP BA5S

NAME_____

ADDRESS_____APT._____

CITY_____

STATE_____ZIP_____

Offer limited to one per household and not valid for present subscribers. Prices subject to change.

PRINTED IN U.S.A.

As a Harlequin Subscriber, you'll receive free . . .

- our monthly newsletter
  HEART TO HEART
- our magazine
  ROMANCE DIGEST
- bonus books and gifts
- special edition Harlequin Best Sellers to
  preview for 10 days without obligation

DETACH AND MAIL TODAY

RUSH

BUSINESS REPLY CARD

First Class   Permit No. 70   Tempe, AZ

Postage will be paid by addressee

Harlequin Reader Service
2504 W. Southern Avenue
Tempe, Arizona 85282

NO POSTAGE
NECESSARY
IF MAILED
IN THE
UNITED STATES

other side there's usually a calm bay where it's safe to swim.'

'Are we visiting this one?' she was catching odd glimpses of land through the spray.

'No,' he steered well clear of it, 'we're going further on.'

The island they arrived at was far out in the Caribbean with no difficult reef to negotiate. There was a sheltered bay, however, and its white beaches were backed by low hills.

Neale gazed with delight as Lawton dropped anchor. 'Beautiful!' she breathed. 'Is it deserted?'

'I've never seen anyone.'

This suggestion that he came here often brought a tiny frown to her face. 'You know it well?'

'I know these waters well,' he amended. 'Years ago I sometimes called here when I had a particular problem.'

'Not a blonde one?'

His eyes teased. 'You're the first woman I ever brought here. I used to believe the place had magical qualities.'

Was there some connection? 'You usually found an answer?'

'I can't have been here for ten years. I learnt to make my own decisions.'

She could believe it. It was difficult to believe he hadn't always been able to. As they waded ashore, she glanced at him sideways. 'You must have been to the Caribbean recently? People recognise you immediately.'

'Of course,' he pulled her the last yards to the fine, sandy beach. 'I have property all over the Caribbean, mostly in Barbados. But that's business—which I want to forget for a few days.'

Letting herself be charmed by the persuasion in his voice, she met the warmth of his eyes, without her usual caution. The island, even life, suddenly exhilarated her, bringing a sparkle to her vivid features. It was so difficult not to respond to the lightness of the

atmosphere and the man by her side that she didn't
even try.

They might have been alone in the world. All around
was only huge wastes of sea and sky, not another
person in sight. The beach was crescent-shaped, nestling
under the protection of the hills. The air was warm and
soft, like silk. Neale thought of the coolness of autumn
at home and shivered.

'What was that about?' Lawton was busy spreading a
rug he had brought from the boat but he never missed
anything.

She laughed ruefully. 'I was thinking how different
the weather is in England.'

'Enjoy this while you can,' he grinned. 'The sea is
warm too. Are you going to swim?'

It would be a pity not to make the most of such an
opportunity. He began removing his shirt and she
averted her eyes, an odd shyness overwhelming her as
she took off her shorts. Next she struggled with her top,
which was tight and threatened to take her bikini with
it.

As she tried to remove one without the other, she
heard Lawton pause. There was amusement in his voice
as he asked mockingly, 'Having trouble?'

'No!' she choked between her teeth, 'you go on, I'll
follow. I can manage on my own.'

In another moment her top was whipped off, and
because he wasn't gentle she considered she was lucky
that her bikini was still in place. 'If you tell me again,'
he said bitingly, 'that I'm not needed, you'll suffer
worse than a little lost dignity.'

Neale quivered with anger as he added insult to injury
by letting his eyes roam every inch of her figure. Her
heart began beating rapidly but she felt worse when she
looked at him. The sight of him in brief trunks made
her cheeks grow hot. Her glance was riveted on his
powerful frame and she couldn't look away.

He didn't attempt to take her in his arms but laid a

finger on the rapidly beating pulse in her throat, then trailed it down to the hard tip of a breast. 'Are you trying to pretend I don't affect you?' he asked softly.

His mockery taunted her. He was too experienced not to know exactly what was happening to her. She could feel a deep trembling starting in her limbs and, with the instincts of a small, feline animal, knew she might have mere seconds to escape him.

With a strangled cry she turned and fled, not waiting for him as she plunged into the sea. It was devastating to learn she was no longer even reasonably indifferent to his blatant masculinity. The potent effect he had on her filled her with apprehension as she failed to understand the fierceness of her own reactions. She felt the warmth and passion throbbing through her was a direct betrayal of the cold indifference that had kept her so well protected from men over the years. Useless to pretend she wasn't vulnerable; she had known this each time he kissed her. Today, though, had been terrifyingly different. He had only touched her briefly, yet had shown her an entirely new concept of herself. She was devastated to suspect that if they ever made love, her response to him might be entirely abandoned.

A good swimmer, she dived deeply below the sea's placid surface, grateful for its cooling effect. The water was buoyant and these qualities instilled in her mind, reducing that which worried her to minor proportions. Her hair, streaming behind her, was a perfect foil for her lissom body, and when a strand of it got in her eyes and she brushed it aside, she saw Lawton following her.

His limbs, much more powerful than hers, shortened the distance between them swiftly, but she didn't mind. Her heart leapt again and a wild kind of recklessness possessed her, making her suddenly careless of what might happen.

He was beside her when she surfaced but not touching. This gave her confidence. 'Those fish, Lawton!' her eyes sparkled with pleasure. 'I know I mentioned them before but I never dreamt there were as many—and in such wonderful colours.'

'The artist in you can't get over it?' he tossed the wet hair from his face. 'You must have read about them, as well as coral reefs?'

'Of course,' she said indignantly, 'but reality beats books anytime.'

He nodded wryly. 'At least your enthusiasm's refreshing. It turns you into an entirely different girl. How about sparing a bit for me?'

'We were discussing fish.'

'Am I not a big enough one?'

Not liking the way he said that, she glared at him angrily. 'Perhaps not,' she taunted.

Her defiance irritated him. 'Little fool!' he exclaimed. 'I was looking at you. Don't you realise what an enchanting picture you make? You're so slender yet you have exactly the right curves in the right places. I couldn't keep my eyes off you. I wanted to make love to you, right there on the sea-bed, but you didn't spare me a glance. You were absorbed in those damned fish, and you expect me to admire them!'

'Lawton, please!' she had been going to rave at him but finding her cheeks scarlet and frightened of what he might read from them, she dived from him again. She had hoped he had forgotten about making love. It confused her terribly to discover he hadn't. He was seducing her with words, without conscience, and she wondered how long she could resist him?

He was waiting when she came up the second time, and, as a wave washed her unexpectedly nearer, he caught her to him, dropping a brief salute on her startled lips. She thought he was letting her go but as her mouth quivered his hold tightened and he gathered her against the roughness of his chest. When she stiffened in protest, his fingers burrowed in her wet hair, stilling her struggles as he deepened the kiss.

Her lips parted under the demanding pressure of his,

the blood drumming in her ears. Voluntarily she strained towards him, suddenly overcome by a feverish longing to be closer still. There was heady stimulation to be found in the merging of their two bodies. Every one of his muscles was imposing on her, making her flesh melt. Every touch, every caress sent her soaring to incredible heights and reality began slipping away.

It wasn't until his hand began exploring her breasts that she dimly realised what was happening and ghosts from the past returned to haunt her. Tony had wanted her, as Lawton did. His hands, too, had roamed over her, seeking his own satisfaction. Men were all alike—only after one thing!

She drew back, just as Lawton began untying the straps of her bikini. He must have thought she was trying to help him, for he murmured huskily, 'Getting impatient, too, my darling?'

The implication that she couldn't wait, shocked her. Taking him by surprise, she jerked free of his possessive hands. 'I'm hungry, Lawton.'

He made no attempt to detain her. He didn't move but his eyes narrowed as he saw the alarm on her face. 'Wouldn't it be more honest to say you're scared?'

Colour ran under her cheeks as she paused guiltily, but she didn't try to evade the truth again. 'You could be right,' she confessed.

To her surprise his face softened and instead of the lecture she expected, he said quite gently, 'Stop worrying, Neale. I know you have this hangover but we've enough time. Perhaps lunch wouldn't be a bad idea, after all. You have to get used to the idea of belonging to me.'

Was he talking about a postponement of hours or days? Neale trailed after him unhappily as he walked out of the water and up the beach. There was no contempt in his eyes but she was just as afraid of his patience. It had been a mistake to promise him anything and she'd been a fool to hope he wouldn't remember. Each time he kissed her she was aware of her own vulnerability. It grew increasingly impossible, when she was in his arms, to retain even a modicum of common sense, and once she gave in to him, would she ever be able to live without him? Men like Lawton Baillie left their own special stamp. For a woman it might mean either ecstasy or devastation!

Their picnic was delicous, chicken and lobster with fresh rolls and cheese, washed down with white wine. For dessert they ate fresh strawberries which Neale was sure tasted of nectar. There was even a flask of hot coffee to end a feast fit for a king.

Afterwards Neale was so replete with good food and wine that when Lawton asked if she would like to explore the island, she declined. 'I don't think I would get very far,' she laughed, ruefully rubbing her flat stomach. 'I fear I've made a pig of myself.'

'We'd have offended the galley if we'd taken anything back,' he said lazily.

'The seagulls have enjoyed it too,' she observed wryly, throwing them the last of the scraps. 'They're the same, the world over, aren't they? Greedy birds.'

Lawton leaned back on the slight incline, pillowing his head in his arms. 'They aren't all seagulls,' he murmured.

Instantly diverted, she saw at once he was right. There were other species among the ones she was familiar with. She watched them for a few minutes and was just about to ask their names when her glance was caught by a flutter of vivid colour in the tree spreading it's huge branches above them. 'Oh, look!' she cried eagerly, 'Isn't that a parrot?'

But Lawton was fast asleep. He had once told her he could drop off instantly and found it handy to be able to refresh himself this way during a twenty-four hour day. Feeling astonishingly resentful that he should have cut himself off from her so deliberately, she considered wandering along the shore for an hour or two. Then she decided she might be wiser to have a sleep as well, as she could scarcely keep her own eyes open.

When she woke, an hour later, he was still sleeping and she studied him for luxurious moments, unobserved. In sleep some of the hardness had left his face but his features were too forcefully hewn ever to be softened completely. While she had, much to his taunting amusement, wrapped herself in a huge towel for lunch, he had refused to do any other but stay as he was. Now she took unashamed advantage of his decision by allowing her slumberous glance to wander freely over the magnificent proportions of his figure. It wasn't the first time she had noticed the breadth of his shoulders and back, the bulging thigh muscles beneath the lean waist, but it was the first time she had seen him asleep and hadn't felt compelled to avert her eyes. He was like a Greek god.

Her cheeks pink, her heart beating rapidly, she scrambled to her feet. Trying to blame the lingering effects of the wine they had drank at lunch for the unsteadiness of her legs, she stumbled towards the sea. Nothing like a cool dip for knocking sense into a crazy mind!

She had waded to her waist, just about to dive, when Lawton caught her. Feeling his hands on her and knowing it could only be him, she wasn't so much frightened as alarmed as he swung her into his arms and carried her back on shore.

'I was going for another swim!' she protested, managing to find her voice as he dumped her on the rug, 'You were asleep.'

His steely eyes glinted. 'It must have been the noise you made. I thought you were going to take off.'

'I'm sorry if I woke you,' she muttered, convinced she hadn't made a sound, 'but there was no need to bring me back. I was in no danger.'

'You think you'd be safer in the sea than with me?' he teased, dropping down beside her. 'What if a shark got you?'

'Would you mind?' moving an inch away from him, she reached for a towel to dry her wet legs.

'Not if I'd had you first,' he growled, taking the towel from her and continuing the job himself.

Her pulse throbbed a warning and she had to force herself to endure his ministrations. All her instincts told her to run, while she could, but she feared that opposition would only make him more determined.

He swept the towel to her feet, accidentally catching her toes, making her giggle. 'Nothing wrong with some of your responses,' he laughed, throwing the towel away and pushing her back, easing himself alongside her. Their faces were only inches apart and as their eyes met the laughter died. 'Neale?' he murmured.

A potent sensation of delight swept through her as he put a hand to the nape of her neck and she waited breathlessly for his kiss. His head came down, blotting out light as she experienced again the sensual magic of his lips. Closing her eyes, she breathed in sharply, catching the masculine smell of him, virile and warm. Awareness shivered along her nerve ends as his mouth moved hungrily over hers, parting its softness, exploring its sweet depth. She seemed to be catching on fire with an aching fever which made her skin burn.

As his kisses grew more passionate, the melting force of his ardour sent her arms tightly round him and with a growl of triumph deep in his throat, Lawton began to undress her. This time she made no demur as he undid the top of her bikini and he feasted his eyes on the soft, rounded contours of her breasts.

'You're beautiful!' he groaned, cupping them lovingly in his hands. Her nipples went taut as his tongue touched them and his teeth bit gently. 'You want me, don't you?' he muttered, 'I can tell.'

If he knew what was happening to her, Neale didn't. Her mind was functioning at a low ebb, dominated by the overwhelming needs of her body. She heard her voice whispering, yes, and knew the answer hadn't

come from her head, but was quite willing to go along
with it.

That she had openly acknowledged her longing for
him seemed to release a hidden spring in her body.
Nothing existed but the desire to give herself. Her
insides were clenched in sweet agony, impatient to
absorb him into her flesh, to belong to him and have
him belonging to her completely. 'Oh, Lawton, I can't
wait,' she groaned. 'Please love me.'

'In a moment,' he promised thickly, his eyes taking in
every female inch of her, sending fire coursing through
her veins. She had never belonged to another man and
she was vaguely aware that she should tell him but
somehow the words wouldn't come.

His body, hardening against her, told her he was as
impatient as she was but he still took his time. His
mouth, warm and moist, descended again on hers,
tasting the heat of her lips before trailing to the
throbbing curve of her throat then on to the swelling
thrust of her breasts. And all the while his hands
roamed over her, caressing and exciting her to a point
near to frenzy.

It wasn't until with a shuddering breath he removed
her bikini briefs and rolled on top of her that the weight
of him brought her momentarily to her senses. Yet the
quick shiver of virginal fright that rushed over her as he
parted her legs, might have made little impact if a
seagull, perhaps hoping for more food, hadn't
squawked loudly beside them.

Her eyes flew wide open. There was a flame like glow
in Lawton's as, making no attempt to hide his passion,
he started kissing her again, but the spell was broken
and she began to struggle frantically.

'Darling,' Lawton said hoarsely, as her struggles
began getting through to him. 'What's wrong? What is
it, Neale?'

Somehow she had to escape this madness consuming
her before it was too late. Squirming, she managed to

get from under him, deafening her ears and senses to his persuasive hands and coaxing tones. Grabbing her bikini, she began dressing, shaking her head in mute agony when he jumped to his feet beside her and asked her roughly what she thought she was doing?

'W—what does it look like——' she choked.

He couldn't seem to believe she was serious. Putting his arms round her, he pulled her back against his chest, nuzzling her neck with hot lips, cupping her breasts with his hands. Suddenly, feeling the hardness of his arousal, she realised he was naked, and clawed desperately at his hands as her traitorous body began to respond.

'No, let me go!' she cried, twisting away from him.

She put only a hair's breadth between them when he swung her savagely back. 'You can't mean that?'

It was impossible to look at him, with all her senses screaming for her to give in. She had to concentrate heavily on Tony and his treachery before she could find the strength to nod.

'But—why?' he muttered tightly, between clenched teeth. 'For God's sake why?'

What could she say to him? What could she tell him that he didn't already know? Soon the frozen feeling would return to protect her but until then she had to be careful. She was standing on the familiar precipice, the yawning chasm, which she could reach but daren't jump over. Not since Tony had she been tempted to, and with him she had never known temptation like this. But Lawton would treat her just as Tony had done and she would never voluntarily go through that again!

She became aware of Lawton's arms urging her gently. 'This makes no sense, darling, when we want each other.'

She hadn't been able to hide how much she had wanted him. It was useless to deny it for he knew. He could make her pulses race, her whole being throb with desire. The deep freeze still existed, but if they hadn't been interrupted she might have belonged to him by now. It seemed the hand of fate might have saved her, from what might have been a taste of sheer heaven, but hell later!

Drawing courage from a deep breath, she said tautly, 'I'm sorry.'

His fingers bit cruelly into her shoulders, his eyes black fires of contempt. 'I guess you're more familiar with the old clichés regarding a situation like this than I am, so I won't quote them to you. But the next time you give a man promises you have no intention of fulfilling, just pray that he will let you off as lightly as I have. Now let's go.'

Tears glistened in Neale's eyes as she numbly watched him repacking their picnic things. She had no defence, he hadn't accused illogically, she was guilty of everything he said. He picked up the towels and hamper and she stumbled after him to the launch. He didn't help her aboard, nor did he speak to her during the whole of the journey back. After a while some of the rigidness that spoke of anger left his shoulders but was replaced by an aura of cool indifference. While Neale sat and shivered, frequently having to bite her lip to prevent herself from breaking down completely, he gazed idly in front of him, never sparing her a glance.

It was pretty obvious he had already dismissed her as a regrettable case of misjudgment. His only interest in her had been sexual. She should be congratulating herself that she hadn't given in to him, instead of weeping inside.

Freddy and Brian were sunning themselves on deck when they returned to the yacht. Coming from the island, it hadn't seemed to matter that Lawton ignored her, but, here, she found it humiliating. Trying not to notice the raised eyebrows as he didn't even look round once to see how she was managing, she scrambled from the launch as best as she could and went straight to her cabin.

There was only an hour to dinner and while she didn't feel hungry, she had no desire that Lawton should believe she was sulking. Even if it killed her, she would get ready and try and eat something!

Throwing off her sandy clothes, she showered then lay on her bed, wearily attempting to bring some order to her mind. Tomorrow she must ask Lawton—beg him, if necessary—to look at the work she had brought, then see if she couldn't book a flight home. After what had happened this afternoon, he couldn't possibly want her to stay.

Her decision made, Neale found her white slacks and a silky blouse and began dressing. She would never have guessed that being in love could make her feel so miserable. She should have known from her previous experience with Tony what might happen but it was difficult to imagine that falling in love a second time could be worse. Brushing her hair, she used more make-up than usual to hide the paleness of her cheeks then went quietly to join the others in the saloon.

'Did you have a good time today?' June enquired brightly as she walked in. They were all drinking when Neale appeared and June glanced at her consideringly over the rim of her glass. 'You look worn out, poor child. I've often told Lawton he doesn't realise his own energy.'

Lawton gave every indication of being blind and deaf. He left it to Freddy to ask what Neale wanted to drink?

Evonne's eyes gleamed maliciously. 'Poor darling, he looks like he's been bored stiff,' she murmured softly, and Neale flushed painfully when Lawton made no attempt to deny it.

Lawton's bad mood lasted throughout dinner, putting a damper on the company. After coffee, believing she was responsible for it, Neale asked to be excused. When Freddy protested, she tried to laugh lightly. 'I'm not used to so much sea and sun.'

Everyone said goodnight except Lawton, who added to her misery by merely glancing at her grimly.

She was up early next morning, seeking him out. He wasn't having breakfast but she found him in his office, thankfully alone. The tray of coffee and toast beside him was evidence that he had been working for some time.

'Come in, Neale, and sit down,' he said when she knocked.

She gazed at him unhappily. He didn't seem angry, this morning, and somehow she hated herself for disappointing him. Deep yearnings penetrated the armour round her heart, reinforced during the night. If she had let him make love to her, would she have felt so anguished this morning?

'Have you eaten yet?'

His voice was quite kindly, surprising her again. When she shook her head and murmured she had thought it more important to see him, he waved her to the chair she still hadn't taken and poured her a cup of coffee.

'I wanted to see you as well,' he said. 'But you go first.'

Nervously, she pushed at her hair, though she wasn't wearing it loose, a fact he noted without comment. 'I wonder if you would have time to look over the work I brought? Then, if there are any further changes, I can make a note of them and go home.'

Her halting request was acknowledged with a slow inclination of his head. He appeared quite willing. 'We could go through it this afternoon, and I can think about it overnight. You should be able to return to the UK within the next forty-eight hours.'

As she frowned uncertainly, unsure whether this was good news or bad, he asked shrewdly, 'Is it work that's worrying you, Neale, or something else?'

'Chiefly work,' she lied.

Bending a glance on her pale face and smudged eyes,

he said curtly. 'If it's me, I want to tell you there's no need.' He paused before continuing gently, 'I've been thinking things over and I realise I haven't been fair. I've been trying to force you into a situation you don't want. I realise your late fiancé's influence on your life is much greater than mine could ever be, and if you're happy the way you are, then who am I to try and inflict my will on you? From now on, Neale, you have nothing to fear from me.'

Where were the feelings of relief? Why did she only feel despair? Lowering her eyes, she tried to ignore the increasing ache in her heart, bewildered by what she could only view as her own contrariness. The reasons Lawton put forward for ending their friendship were sound. He wasn't a man who would have any use for a static relationship. If it failed to develop the way he expected, he would prefer a clean break. And who could blame him? There would be plenty of other women available who wouldn't know what it meant to be inhibited.

'Thank you,' she whispered, managing to insert some of the gratitude he appeared to be waiting for into her voice.

He nodded, the subject apparently closed. 'June wants to wander round the town. She's an inveterate shopper and you might like to take the opportunity of finding a few things for yourself. Then, after lunch, we will get down to work.'

Neale hadn't thought, after feeling so depressed, that she would find the morning such fun. They roamed about the market, full of small farmers and stallholders, selling everything including all kinds of fruit and foodstuffs. From there they proceeded to Bridge Street, where most of the largest shops were. Lawton, soon tiring of shopping, left Brian in charge of his wife and June and took Neale and Freddy off to Jeremie Street insisting, to Neale's surprise, that she must visit the Home Industries Centre. She was, in fact, enchanted by the range of straw hats and bags, cane chairs, sisal rugs and goods too numerous to browse through in one go. When they left, her face was glowing with the enthusiasm which could make her look so radiant and she didn't see Lawton glancing at her grimly.

Eventually Lawton sent Freddy to fetch the others in a taxi while he and Neale did the journey to Morne Fortune in a donkey cart, where he decided they would all have lunch.

Neale had argued with herself against asking Lawton to take her for a donkey ride but, in the end, she had been unable to resist it. After all it was her last day and there were enough people about. It wasn't as though they would be entirely alone.

Lawton had agreed wryly, but the brief qualm she felt soon disappeared as the fun mounted. Morne Fortune was the height just behind Castries, on whose crest stands Fort Charlotte, an eighteenth-century fortress that changed hands about a dozen times during the years of English–French colonial warfare. The donkey was nothing if not erratic, alternating between bursts of speed and sudden halts, much to the annoyance of its driver. In some countries donkeys are treated cruelly but here persuasion seemed more a matter of raising and lowering the voice and waving hands. By the time they reached the restaurant, Neale was giggling irrepressibly and she and Lawton were walking behind the cart instead of in it.

'I hope you thought it was worth it?' Lawton said sternly, as he paid off the driver and Neale wiped tears of mirth from her cheeks. Yet as he handed her back the straw hat she had bought but lost during their journey, a reluctant smile tugged the edges of his firm mouth.

They ate well at a restaurant overlooking the city. Neale was entranced with the view and wished she'd had time to explore the whole island. She didn't mention this, of course, as she was going home tomorrow and she would hate Lawton to think she was angling for an invitation to stay longer.

It was late when they finished and she was beginning to get anxious as they returned to the yacht. Lawton, however, hadn't forgotten his promise. After a short interlude he sent a steward to tell her he was ready to begin work.

Later, when she had explained, and he had considered everything, he said he would think it over and let her know. It was exactly what he had told her earlier, so she wasn't disappointed at not getting his immediate approval. She was sure this would come. He had seemed relatively satisfied and she was relieved to have got as far as this.

Impulsively she decided not to dress for dinner. After leaving Lawton's office, she had returned to her cabin and because she was tired, had fallen asleep. When she woke she was startled to see that she didn't hurry she would be late. After showering quickly, she scrambled into her white slacks and rushed to the saloon.

It was empty, apart from the steward waiting to serve her her meal. Lawton, she was informed, on gathering sufficient courage to ask, had gone out with the others to a party and it wasn't known when they would be back.

The food she was served was delicous but she found she could scarcely eat a thing. As soon as she felt she reasonably could, she went back to her quarters, racked by spasms of pain. Already Lawton was showing her he meant what he said. From now on she would be kept in her place, and as it was the place she herself had chosen, how could she complain? After this he would regard her merely as an employee, and, as such, she must not expect to have the pleasure of his company in anything that wasn't connected with business. With a groan, Neale flung herself on her bed and began to weep.

CHAPTER SEVEN

THE pain was terrible, giving her no rest. After a while she rose, rinsed her tear-drenched face and went up on deck. Apart from a sailor on watch, the yacht seemed deserted and she stood for a time gazing seaward, past the outline of the city, clearly visible beneath a canopy of stars.

Eventually, after a cooling breeze had soothed her hot cheeks, she retraced her footsteps down below and prepared for bed. She felt calmer and it didn't seem to matter so much that her eyes were faintly red. Brushing her hair until it floated loosely about her shoulders, which relieved her aching head, with a sigh she pulled on her thin nightdress and crawled under the single sheet. Nothing ever appeared to be as bad in the morning, it was said.

After a period of restlessness, she was drowsing when her cabin door opened and Lawton walked in, closing it behind him. Her eyes widened as she saw he was wearing his dressing-gown, a rather magnificent affair which in no way detracted from his air of authority. For a moment surprise held her silent, then, as he made no attempt to explain his presence, she whispered huskily, 'I thought you had gone to a party?'

He came nearer and stood looking down at her. 'That's one of the reasons I'm here,' he said obliquely. 'Another was—your plans. I believed if I didn't let you know I can find no fault with them this time, you wouldn't sleep.'

Neale felt too numb to feel any great reaction, but, because he had been kind enough to come and tell her, she forced a smile. It must have been a wobbly effort for he suddenly frowned and sat down beside her.

'Don't worry,' he said wearily as she visibly stiffened, 'I'm not thinking of seducing you. I'm concerned, that's all. You've been crying?'

'Something got in my eye, on deck,' she muttered, wondering how many more white lies she would tell before she was free of him. 'You don't have to bother.'

'Damn it all, Neale!' he exclaimed under his breath, 'I do bother! That's the hardest part of it. You've got under my skin, a little slip of a thing like you, and I can't get any of the old cures to work.'

She frowned, not following, and not sure that she wanted to. It didn't seem to matter that the sheet was practically around her waist, and that her silky nightdress couldn't be hiding much. Despite the odd things he said, she felt sure she had nothing to fear from him, except, perhaps, his total disinterest.

'You've been out, this evening,' she remarked, without realising how desolate she sounded.

He sighed, watching her thoughtfully. 'I came to see if you wanted to come but you were asleep and I hadn't the heart to wake you. Not for the kind of party we were going to anyway.'

Immediately Neale felt warmer and it showed. A little of the unhappiness left her face and her eyes glowed softly. 'You didn't stay long?'

'No,' he confessed grimly, 'I wasn't in the mood. It will probably be daybreak before the others return, though.'

Questions tumbled through her mind in less than the space of a breath and she asked the first one that entered her head. 'Weren't you enjoying yourself?'

'Haven't I just told you?'

As she nodded, his mouth quirked wryly. 'Do you know, darling, I had a better time this morning, on—or was it pushing? that donkey cart.'

She had to convince herself that the darling was purely incidental. 'I enjoyed it too,' impulsively she touched his hand with eager fingers. 'Thank you.'

He stared intently into her shy, shining eyes. 'Don't you realise, Neale, that when you're out like that, forgetting yourself completely, you're an entirely different person? You're so natural and full of fun, able to find pleasure in simple things, which, believe me, is a priceless asset. And there is so much more you could enjoy if only you'd let yourself. A home, husband and children?'

As she couldn't have him, she didn't want to think about the rest. She swallowed but managed to counter coolly, 'Why haven't you ever married, Lawton?'

'I've never met anyone for whom I'd exchange my freedom,' he shrugged, eyes wary.

He can't believe, she thought bitterly, that I'm trying to trap him? At least she knew her limitations!

'I won't ever marry,' she muttered fiercely, hoping to convince him.

'Neale!' he retorted quietly. 'In saying that, do you really think you're being fair to either yourself or your ex-fiancé? You can't go on believing he has ruined your life. Look,' he took the small hand lying close to his in both his, 'why don't you tell me about it, my sweet?'

She stared at him helplessly, her face degrees paler. 'I—can't.'

He remained impassive, doing nothing to increase her unconscious agitation. The colour was running wildly under her skin, her pupils dilated to an extent which betrayed the strain she was under. 'How about beginning with your schooldays?' he coaxed softly. 'Your parents?'

It was getting worse, she drew a sharp breath. 'No!' she gasped, 'I couldn't possibly!'

Noting her changed breathing, the beads of perspiration on her brow, Lawton's arms went suddenly round her before she could attempt to draw back. 'Come on, Neale,' he growled, his voice gentle but inflexible, 'it's not something you can bottle up forever.'

She tried to fight him but his arms were persuasive and she had never expected to have them around her

again. With a sob she relaxed against him as his
kindness proved too much for her. She began telling
him little things, then couldn't seem to stop.

She told him, though, more about where she had
lived than the drawbacks of having professional parents
who thought their careers much more important than
their only child. It was left to Lawton to read between
the lines. He held her close but not too tightly and each
time she paused he prompted her gently to go on.

'My broken engagement was a great blow for them,'
she revealed, her voice trembling. 'You see, all the
arrangements were made for them to emigrate to
Australia and their plans didn't include me.'

'Hadn't they allowed that something might happen?'

Neale didn't see the angry gleam in his eyes for her
face was hidden against him. 'No. . . . Anyway,' she
confessed honestly, 'I had no desire to go with them.
After Tony left me I only wanted to get my degree and
begin working.'

'How often have you seen them since they went?'
Lawton asked, stroking the rumpled hair from off her
hot forehead.

She sighed, 'They haven't been back, but we write.'

His mouth thinned but his hands were gentle on her
shoulders and he began pressing comforting kisses
along her brow. She trembled, but recognised his
caresses as merely compassionate and didn't pull away.
His hands were very soothing, too, massaging some of
the tension from her nape. Beginning to like the way
they moved over her, she snuggled closer to his hard
body, feeling a wonderful sense of ease. He asked
questions and listened to her halting replies without
criticism, which somehow encouraged her to continue.
She had never mentioned her family in years. In the
office, a lot of the staff mightn't know she had one.

Lawton turned her face gently up towards him, to
accommodate his kisses better. 'How long after you and
Tony broke up did they stay with you?'

'About a week.'

'And you so young!'

It was the first hint of stricture she had detected but she didn't feel resentful. His arms and lips were like a drug, deadening the adverse effects of her confession.

He was silent for a moment then said softly. 'What was it about your broken engagement that had such a lasting effect?'

She had began to believe he had forgotten about her engagement and couldn't prevent a shiver of coldness from running right through her. 'Please!' she faltered, but when he was adamant, she gave in, telling him what he wanted to know, speaking huskily between short, painful breaths.

'It wasn't just that Tony changed his mind,' she confessed. 'Everyone is entitled to do that, but he left me standing at the altar, just like in the song. I was waiting at the church and he didn't turn up.' Now she was really shuddering, her body racked as she clung to Lawton wildly. 'It was dreadful, that's why I can't ever trust another man! Not only did Tony never send word that he wasn't coming to our wedding, but the night before, when he knew he was in love with another girl, he visited me, while my parents were out, and— and. . . .'

'Hush, darling,' Lawton cut her off, his voice smothered against the top of her head, and because he had stopped her she found it impossible to go on and began sobbing convulsively.

He let her sob for several minutes until she grew quieter, then he murmured. 'Don't mind me, darling. It's the only way to get it out of your system, to get rid of all the hurt. I take it there hasn't been another man since?'

Blindly Neale shook her glossy head. Her tears were soaking his dressing-gown. He must be glad they had stopped but his arms were so comforting she couldn't pull away. She could actually feel the deep ice that had been so long inside her, permanently dissolving.

Lawton's kisses were still gentle. 'You can't get over that he went straight from you to her?'

'I suppose not,' she admitted, as the familiar chemistry began working between them, dizzying her mind. How could she think of Tony when Lawton was here? She loved Lawton. What she had felt for Tony, she recognised now as childish infatuation. A flutter of desire began low in her stomach and rose to quicken her heart. Without thinking she slid her arms round him, digging her fingers into the hard muscles of his back so that he groaned aloud.

The quality of Lawton's kisses changed. Before his lips had brushed like butterflies, now the pressure altered. Yet there was no sign of undue haste as he tenderly laid her back against the pillows and began slowly removing her nightgown.

As the straps slipped over her shoulders, she stiffened but he soothed her with drugging words, 'Ghosts have to be exorcised, my darling. Trust me.'

She wanted to. Suddenly she knew she had to belong to him. Surrendering to the aching certainty inside her, she closed her eyes against the glowing flames in his as her nightgown was drawn expertly from her trembling body. His dressing-gown followed to the floor and her pulse raced as he tipped up her head to allow his mouth to burn a tantalising trail from her throat to the pink tips of her breasts. Fire leapt through her veins, rendering her limp and vulnerable. Never had she felt so totally feminine, beautiful or desirable as she felt now. As Lawton's warm mouth crushed her lips, not even the bliss she had experienced when they had been alone together on the island seemed as good as this.

All her inhibitions, Tony, all the black clouds that had dogged her for so long, disappeared. Lawton might not love her but he had helped her. If she gave herself to him it would be only just return. And for her it would be a moment out of time, something to remember all her life—the long years when she would be alone. Surely she couldn't be condemned for snatching such a small measure of happiness?

Murmuring how wonderful he found her, Lawton continued kissing and caressing her and the feeling between them reached new heights. It was as though deprivation had sharpened the hunger previously denied. His mouth grew hot and urgent, drawing Neale tumultuously into the web of his passion. Her bemused mind blanked out everything except her awareness of him, the delight of his mouth exploring hers as his solid length strained against her willing body.

His hands moulded her hips and she trembled with excitement as her breasts came in contact with the rough curling hair on his chest. Sensation surged again and she ceased to be conscious of anything but the strong, virile man whose arms she was in. A spreading weakness invaded her limbs as he devastatingly kissed every inch of her, his fingers pressed on her contracting stomach, holding her still while his teeth tugged first at one nipple then another until he interrupted the passionate capture of her breasts to kiss her lower down.

'Let me love you, darling?' he begged softly, raising himself to nuzzle her slender throat.

She nodded dazedly, unable to speak. She felt alight inside, like a forest fire, with no control of the flames. But Lawton, she realised, was the only one who could assuage them. His magnificent maleness filled her with delight and suggested realms of pleasure more miraculous than anything she had ever imagined.

'I want you too, Lawton,' she murmured, when he put a hand under her chin and made her look at him. As their eyes met, she veiled hers shyly with thick lashes, but not before he caught a glimpse of the longing threatening to consume her. . . .

With a groan he rolled on top of her, his urgency no longer restrained. His legs trapped her, as though he feared she might change her mind, while his hands began working down the length of her back, digging into her from the base of her neck to the curve of her thigh. It was like some tender, erotic message and Neale felt herself tremble in response. Convulsively she wrapped her arms around him, feeling the sweat running down his smooth skin. Hearing his breath shudder as she touched him, she was amazed that she could disturb him so.

Then suddenly, as his control gave and he slipped between her legs, she flinched, making him pause. She felt rather than saw him frown but she heard the hoarse surprise in his voice as he asked, 'This will be your first time?'

She had tried to tell him but he hadn't listened, and was immediately apprehensive that he would be angry. He stilled her fears, however, by laying quick fingers over her lips. 'Don't worry, darling. It's too late to stop now, but now that I know, I can make things easier for you.'

'I love you,' she whispered feverishly, not wanting him to stop. She began kissing him of her own accord and with a muffled groan his desire leapt instantly to meet hers and his arms tightened. She was crushed to the mattress by his weight and, for all he was gentle, she barely managed to suppress a scream as he possessed her. Yet, strangely, the pain she experienced brought with it a greater intensity of feeling. As he lifted her fragile body to meet the mounting pressures of his, she clutched him fiercely, letting the waves of his passion carry her higher and higher until the final spiral hurtled them into vibrations of thunderous rapture, ending in incredible joy.

As they floated gently to earth again, Neale lay exhausted in Lawton's arms. When she opened her eyes he was studying her face and she was reassured by the tenderness she saw there. He kissed her gently. 'Thank you, Neale,' he said softly, 'I wanted you very badly but I hope I didn't hurt you?'

'No,' she whispered, wondering, as she smiled at him, if she would ever be so happy again?

He cuddled her closer and ran a teasing finger along her adorable nose. 'I've never felt so satisfied before, my darling.'

For a long time after he fell asleep, Neale refused to think of anything at all but lay quietly under the weight of Lawton's confining arm, listening to his heightened breathing returning to normal. She could find no words to describe what had taken place between them, it was beyond anything she had ever experienced. Together they had surrendered to a primitive passion, as old as man, which had left them lying in a tangle of damp, spent bodies, but whatever happened in the future, she couldn't believe she would ever regret it.

She woke at dawn to find herself still in his arms and a faint panic stirred as she found him watching her lazily. 'I was just about to wake you with a kiss, princess,' he growled, his eyes glowing down on her. 'You look beautiful when you're sleeping but I don't think I can wait to have you again, much longer.'

She was contented and drowsy but as he spoke and his hand moved sensuously, the fierce hunger she had known a few hours ago returned overwhelmingly. She smiled, responding like a little cat, until she lifted her arms and suddenly realised they were both naked.

'And you're in my bed!' she gasped, alarm replacing the desire in her eyes. 'Hadn't you better return to your own cabin while there's time? The steward always brings me morning tea.'

'Shall I ask him to bring mine here as well?' he teased, but when she gazed at him anxiously, he told her gently to stop worrying. 'The crew is well trained, darling. No one's going to think a thing.'

'It—it bothers me though,' a tiny frown creased her brow as her cheeks coloured warmly.

He ran his fingers through her golden hair. 'Darling,' he muttered, 'when you give a man a taste of paradise, you can't be surprised when he wants more. You're enchanting.'

As he turned her on her back and began kissing her again, she tried to resist, for she couldn't share his indifference of other peoples' opinions, but Lawton's possessive ardour proved too much for her, and when he started making love to her, she gave herself up without restraint to the exquisite dictates of his will.

When she woke for the second time, she was alone and she lay for a few minutes thinking of all that had happened to her since yesterday. Yesterday morning she had felt miserable, today she was happy, so happy she actually felt like singing, Lawton had shown her a new world and she was immeasurably grateful. As well as filling her with contentment, she could never recall waking up feeling so carefree. Lawton was right, the spectre of Tony had had to be demolished. Now it was gone she felt a different person. Lawton might not love her but hadn't she enough love for the two of them?

Happiness gave her a vivid radiance which she was sure was too noticeable. As she dressed and ran eagerly to the saloon she did her best to calm down.

Lawton was there with his guests but he had finished eating. When Neale appeared, he rose immediately to escort her to her chair. 'You're late this morning,' he teased, his eyes riveted on her glowing face. 'Are you feeling all right?'

'Of course, she is,' Freddy quipped, dryly, adding, 'You never make a fuss over me!'

Neale, wishing she could get rid of the habit of blushing, glanced shyly at Lawton as she nodded. 'Yes, thank you.'

He poured her coffee himself then pulled a chair up next to her, making sure she had enough to eat. After she had spoken to the others and endured a few curious glances, he said happily, 'We're going sailing today. In fact I believe we're moving now.'

'Oh, where?' she turned to smile at him and somehow got lost in his gaze.

'Not far,' he smiled. 'I want to show you the small island I've purchased. I'm going to turn it into either a home or a holiday centre. I haven't made my mind up yet. It will depend.'

His eyes were telling her something but she was too bemused with pleasure to wonder what it was. The day unfurled gloriously, especially when he kept putting an arm round her and dropping affectionate little kisses on her brow and cheeks. He didn't seem to care who was around or that the attention they were receiving grew increasingly speculative.

The island was a dream. When Lawton had first told her, she had suspected it was the one he had already taken her to, but she soon saw they were travelling in the opposite direction. This one was larger, and he said it would lend itself to several things, depending on his decision.

They all went ashore and another boat followed later with a wonderful lunch. As Neale looked around, her eyes were full of dreams and just a fleeting regret.

'Do I detect a note of sadness?' Lawton came to where he had ordered her to sit, followed by a steward with two heaped plates.

'No—well,' she confessed, accepting her lunch with a smile of appreciation for the young man who had brought it and waiting until he had gone, 'I was thinking, if I hadn't been so foolish, our picnic, the other day, might have had a different ending?'

He bent and kissed her before they started to eat. 'That's because if I wait I'll probably taste of mayonnaise, and, secondly, because I don't want you having any more regrets. From now on we will concentrate on the future.'

It seemed to Neale that the day and night that followed was one of the happiest periods of her life. They spent a wonderful time exploring the island, swimming in the warm sea and generally lapping up all the lovely sun and fresh air.

Lawton insisted, with the exclusion of June, whom he appointed umpire, on playing leap-frog on the beach and Neale nearly made herself ill trying not to laugh at Evonne's antics as she attempted to take part in the hilarious game without losing her dignity. Lawton seemed an entirely different person, his laugher rang out and he looked amazingly carefree, years younger. If he occasionally glanced at Neale broodingly, she didn't see it.

He finished the day by building huge sandcastles, his energy boundless. Then he declared he must have someone to cover up. No one but Neale volunteered and she said cheekily she was only doing it to please him. For having the nerve to laugh at him, he declared severely that if she didn't wish to be made redundant, she must be prepared to pay a forfeit before he freed her from the ton of sand. When he decided the penalty should be a kiss, she pretended to be reluctant but when his lips touched hers, if her arms hadn't been trapped she knew they would have gone round his neck.

That night he came again to her bed and stayed until morning. He was a wonderful lover, able to render her almost mindless with desire then to give her incredible pleasure. She lost all sense of restraint as she gave herself up to the dangerous excitement of his passion, responding with a fevour which, in turn, seemed to excite him.

After they had made love the second time, he confessed that until the previous evening, he had believed she was experienced. Not that she was promiscuous, but he had thought she'd belonged to her fiancé. When he had discovered she was innocent, he had been curious but hadn't questioned her about it for fear of disturbing her too much.

'Would you like to tell me about it now?' he asked, so tenderly that she was encouraged, losing the quick sense of fear she felt when he mentioned it.

'Tony came to me, as I told you,' she whispered huskily. 'He begged me to let him love me, he said it wouldn't matter when we were getting married next day. I almost gave in to him. I realise if I'd been really in love with him I might not have had the strength to resist him. This was what I was trying to explain. I think it was the shock of his behaviour that made me like I was. I was determined never to get close to a man again.'

Lawton's arms tightened protectively as he muttered grimly. 'He acted despicably but you have to remember he's only one man.'

'Yes,' she snuggled into him humbly.

'What I can't understand is why you agreed to meet him when he came to London?'

Because one of Neale's hands was unconsciously caressing his face, she felt the sudden frown on his intelligent forehead. 'When he rang, I wasn't going to. Then he didn't seem important any more. I was so amazed that I suddenly had to see him to convince myself it was true.'

'And was it?'

Lawton's voice was casual, not giving the impression that her answer was so important. How could she answer him? She had seen Tony and discovered he didn't mean a thing, but the ice inside her had been too solidly set to thaw immediately. With a sense of confusion she replied, 'I think so.'

'You don't sound all that sure,' Lawton muttered thickly, 'but I have enough patience.' Then, before she could explain she hadn't meant to appear indecisive, he began kissing her again and she decided hazily to let her responsiveness convince him he was the only one she had ever loved or wanted.

In the morning, before leaving her, he said they would explore St Lucia, just the two of them, alone together. But this was not to be. Neale heard him speaking to someone, just outside her cabin door and soon afterwards he came to inform her they were returning to England.

'There's some trouble concerning a big deal on the continent,' he said briefly, 'I have to go. And unless you'd like to stay on with Freddy and June, I think you'd better come with me.'

She nodded. There was no question of her staying without him. Besides, she ought to get back to work. She was still wearing her silky robe and something in his eyes disturbed her more than his news. It was almost as if he were glad to be going?

Impulsively she murmured. 'You're probably ready to leave, anyway?'

He kept on staring at her but his eyes darkened broodingly, as if he was seeing something else. 'I'm suddenly impatient to get back to London, yes.'

The hurt of his words accompanied her all the way home, though she tried not to take his remark too literally. He might have been thinking solely of business, not anything personal, and certainly he was attentive enough during the journey to banish most of the doubts from her heart.

Rex was gleeful that the plans for the south coast hotel had been passed at last and was eager to get the whole project completed as soon as possible.

'You'd better make a start, Neale,' he said. 'I see that Lawton's made a few amendments but I'm sure you can cope. I'll give you as much help as I can but I'm knee deep in the Spanish job at the moment.'

Mildred wanted to hear all about St Lucia and the boss's yacht. 'Is it as fab as he is?' she giggled.

Neale's smile was softly reminiscent and she flushed as she saw the teasing mockery in Mildred's eyes.

'Did he make a pass at you?' she asked eagerly.

'Mildred! I was working,' Neale retorted sternly.

'What at?' Mildred laughed, sighing, 'I think I'd swoon if he so much as glanced at me!'

'It's a good job we aren't all the same,' Neale

observed dryly. 'Otherwise the decks might have been littered with prostrate bodies. We weren't there alone.'

'Some people never learn to make the most of their opportunities,' Mildred sniffed, and Neale was thankful when the phone began ringing. She feared her hot cheeks were not doing much to convince Mildred that her trip had been as uneventful as she tried to pretend it had been.

Her desk was covered with work but she found it difficult to settle down with half her mind still on the Caribbean. Lawton had flown out again almost immediately and she didn't know how she was going to get through the next few days without him. She wanted him so much she was unable to be happy away from him for a second. Loving Lawton as she did, she felt a constant need to be with him. A need more urgent than anything she had ever known.

Idly she leafed through some papers. From the amount of them, Rex might have guessed she wanted no time to brood. Determined to be sensible, she began working, and the day assumed the usual familiar yet oddly comforting pattern. She contacted wholesalers, arranged for quotations, sent out plans for some of the work to one or two firms of interior decorators, asking for estimates—there was no end to it. All these people would be back to her later for more specialised information and she had to be available to give it to them. The company employed their own teams for most of the basic work but there was always some that called for skills they didn't have available.

It was late when she glanced up to see Lawton's secretary entering her office.

'I'm so glad I caught you,' the woman smiled, 'Mr Baillie gave me this to deliver to you, before you went home.'

An envelope, bulky but small, was placed on her desk, and with a wry grimace about it being cold outside, Miss Hepworth departed.

Always wary of surprises, Neale stared at the envelope curiously. Lawton hadn't promised to ring but she had thought he might. She certainly wasn't expecting a mysterious package which filled her with unaccountable apprehension.

Rex and his secretary were still busy, she could see them through the glass partitions in the adjoining department, but Mildred and the rest of the staff had gone. Suddenly she picked up the envelope, ripping it open, dealing ruthlessly with her foolish fears. It couldn't be a bomb, for heaven's sake! There was something wrapped in tissue. Neale frowned, trying to guess what it was as she unravelled it. It was a key. Gazing at it in bewilderment, she picked up the sheet of paper enclosed with it and began to read.

'This is the key to my apartment, Neale—I want to find you there when I'return. There's the commissionaire but he's an old friend and I've already explained you will be moving in. Until Thursday, my darling. L.M.B.'

He must be asking her to live with him? Neale sat like a small, frozen image, only her hand clenching around the key, giving any indication she was alive. Her face was white and a terrible sickness welled in her throat. She felt shocked and ill.

How could he ever have suggested such a thing? But then, shouldn't she have guessed? While she had trusted Lawton, there had been obvious clues that he was no different from other men. Tightly she closed her eyes as she propped her elbows on the desk and buried her cold face in her hands. All the signs had been there, she must have been blind! No, not blind, she admitted with grim honesty, she had seen them but ignored them!

Lawton didn't love her, he had never even pretended to. He had made love to her which was an entirely different thing. Putting it crudely, he had sampled the goods and liked them and decided he would have her for his mistress. He had given her a key to his apartment so she could be nicely installed when he returned, sparing him any inconvenience. Indisputably she would be handsomely rewarded. After a few weeks, when he tired of her, she would have a cheque thrust in her hands, and he would murmur, with the charming but ruthless smile which she had once or twice seen him using, that their relationship was over.

Oh what a fool she had been! Would she never learn? Neale groaned aloud. Didn't he understand she loved him too much to become his mistress? Her emotions were too involved. Her body craved for him after only two nights spent in his arms. How would it be if she lived with him, became sated with his lovemaking and then was rejected? It might prove a crippling blow from which she might never recover. Better a clean break now, while she still had a chance, than to court complete disaster later.

With numb fingers and ragged breath, she resealed the key with her own letter in another envelope and took a taxi to his apartment. Instructing the driver to wait, she gave the letter to the commissionaire, asking him to make sure that Mr Baillie received it the minute he returned.

On reaching her flat, Neale found she was shaking so badly that she was forced to pour herself a drink of the brandy she usually kept for cooking. Sitting down with it, she sipped it slowly in an attempt to pull herself together. While waiting for its steadying effect, she read Lawton's note again and began reflecting on her own hastily scribbled reply.

She had managed to write:

Dear Mr Baillie, Our holiday romance was a mistake, one which I believe we would both be wiser to forget. I think I'd be happier as I am, concentrating on

*my job and friends. I just don't see myself fitting into
your casual life style. I'm sorry if my decision causes
you any inconvenience but if it does I'm sure you will
soon get over it. Neale Curtis.*

As helplessly as she had done an hour ago in the
office, Neale buried her face in her hands, but, this
time, she tried not to think. She tried to concentrate on
the rain driving against the window instead of the tears
pouring down her cheeks.

After a restless night, she dragged herself to work the
following morning. This was Tuesday, Lawton wouldn't
be back until Thursday. It gave her time, she decided,
to resign herself to the fact that she wouldn't be seeing
him again, yet during the next two days, instead of
feeling calmer, she was so torn by tension that even Rex
noticed she looked ill.

On Thursday afternoon he paused by her desk. 'I'm
beginning to wonder if I haven't given you too much to
do, Neale? I realise the hotel is a big job but I thought
you could cope.'

Rex had enough worries without her adding to them.
'Of course I can cope,' she replied quickly.

He didn't appear altogether convinced. 'I must say
you do look a bit the worse for wear. If you'll forgive
me for saying so,' he added wryly.

Neale smiled wanly. 'I'm probably just suffering from
jet lag, there's no need to worry.'

'Yes, probably you are. Why didn't I think of it?' he
looked relieved. 'I tell you what, why not take
tomorrow off? A long weekend should soon put you
right again.'

About to protest, Neale hesitated then suddenly
agreed. When Lawton returned, if he was angry after
receiving her note, three days should give him time to
cool down. And if she disappeared until Monday, he
might just decide she wasn't worth bothering about?
Whatever happened, he had to be convinced that she

had no desire to become his mistress.

Assuring Rex that she would take a few days off and was very grateful, Neale rushed home to hastily pack a bag and catch the first train she could find going to Shrewsbury. She hadn't been back to the town where she had been born for over four years. She wasn't certain why she was visiting it now, after all this time, but for a day or two it seemed to offer a kind of sanctuary.

Returning to London, late on the Sunday evening, she went straight to bed. Having spent most of the weekend walking and talking to old friends in the frosty country air she was exhausted and slept better than she had done since coming back from the Caribbean. She imagined that Lawton would have given up looking for her by now, if he had ever begun, and she hoped that his pride would be hurting badly enough to make him leave her severely alone!

CHAPTER EIGHT

BEING certain that the long weekend had helped her a lot, Neale was dismayed to find her newly found courage wavering when she reached the office next day.

'Hello, love,' Mildred grinned cheekily. 'You hardly look like an advert for winter breaks, unless it's that you need another one?'

'If you'd shut up for a start, I might feel a whole heap better,' Neale replied in the same vein.

'Typical Monday morning, huh?' Mildred's grin became more sympathetic. 'You're not the only one in a bad mood, by the way. Mr Baillie's rang down twice, personally! You're to get up there—he actually said, here, on the double!'

Neale had to sit down while she willed resentment to replace panic. Mildred knew—as she knew—that Lawton rarely concerned himself to this extent with any member of the design department. At least not like this, first thing in the morning.

Aware that Mildred was looking at her curiously, she asked hoarsely, 'Are you sure he didn't ask for Rex?'

'Not a hope,' her secretary shook her head as the phone buzzed again. 'Yes,' Mildred squeaked into it, 'She's on her way, Mr Baillie.'

'See what I mean?' she mouthed, as Neale fled.

Neale, still overcome by panic, almost rushed straight home again, until she realised, after the first few yards, just how foolish she was being. She would have to face Lawton and hear what he had to say. His bark on the phone suggested if she tried to hide he would find her. He was obviously smarting from her rejection of him and convinced her note couldn't be genuine. Somehow she had to find the courage to convince him it was!

His secretary nearly fell over herself rushing to usher Neale into his office. He was standing beside the window, staring out, his shoulders set rigid. As Neale entered and the door closed behind her, he swung round, transferring his attention to her face.

'Neale!' he exclaimed, swiftly approaching her, his eyes dark with some indefinable emotion and anger. 'Just where the hell have you been? I've worn a path to your door over the weekend. That note you left, I cannot make head nor tail of it! You'll have to explain.'

It could only be chemistry, this awareness that swept through her even when he wasn't touching her. She wished she could look at him and not care or desire any more. The yearning inside her for the taste of his mouth, the bliss of his arms crushing her to him must remain unsatisfied. She must learn to resist temptation, even when it was so near.

Spinning about, she guarded her eyes and tried to pretend an indifference that didn't exist. She still couldn't get the word mistress past her lips so was forced to improvise. 'I should have told you when we left St Lucia,' she mumbled, 'I—I'm not ready for any kind of commitment yet.'

'Neale!' he swung her back to him, holding her anxiously, 'I promised I'd be patient.'

He was drawn, pale under his tan. She tried not to let her bemused eyes explore his tense features but it was difficult not to when he was standing so close to her. Carefully she attempted to ease herself from his hold but found it impossible. He wasn't hurting her but his hands were inexorable.

'You didn't sound very patient.'

'You mean my note? Oh, hell!' he released a hand to tear it in perplexity through his roughened hair, 'I'm sorry about that. I guess I was rushing you but I thought you understood the situation. Can't we make a fresh start, Neale, if I promise not to hurry you this time?'

She had to grit her teeth to prevent her resolve from failing. The drugging male smell of him was driving her mad. 'It would only have the same ending. . . .'

'What other ending did you expect, for heaven's sake?'

'Not good enough,' she muttered, her soft mouth set with determination.

He sighed, his eyes puzzled but suddenly tender as they swept over her. 'You're such a graceful little thing, so much beauty, yet so much stubbornness. What am I going to do with you?'

'Just leave me alone.'

'Oh, damn, damn!' he muttered distractedly, then left her to snarl into the intercom, as his secretary informed him the ministerial delegation was here, that it would have to wait.

Instantly he returned to Neale as if the interruption had never happened. 'I can't leave you alone,' he said heavily, 'I have to wear you down, get you to agree. I could have been wrong about you, but I didn't think you would hesitate.'

It was too much! Anger and pain hit her both at once. Why didn't he just come out with it and ask what higher status than a mistress did a girl like her hope to climb to? Well, she had her pride, as he would learn!

'I'm sorry,' she retorted coldly, 'I find I'm no longer interested.'

'Now you've got rid of your inhibitions,' he shot back, 'you discover you want to play the field? Have you ever considered, but for me, you might still have been cringing in your shell?'

How dared he remind her of that! 'Do you always grab all the credit?' she breathed.

'When it belongs to me, yes. You're mine,' he added menacingly, 'and I'll have you know, I won't tolerate you going out with other men.'

'I can't wait to start!' she retorted, incensed.

'Just get out of here,' he said, so grimly she quailed.

'People are waiting to see you, anyway,' she babbled, stumbling in her haste to obey.

As he grasped an arm to steady her, she heard his breath catch halfway between a rasp and a groan. 'God, Neale!' he exclaimed huskily, 'you've got me in such a state I don't remember what they're here about.'

Neale didn't recall getting from his office back to her own. If Lawton was confused it must be the first time in his life, and he couldn't be nearly as confused as she was. Once she recalled driving, soon after Tony had jilted her, and not being able to remember anything between A and Z. She had been really frightened then, believing she might have had an accident. She felt the same now though there was some comfort to be gained in knowing she'd had only a lift to negotiate instead of a particularly dangerous stretch of motorway.

She worked late that evening, not willing to spend long hours in her flat with only her thoughts for company. How to keep Lawton out of her thoughts was a problem she hadn't yet solved and seeing him again hadn't helped any!

Finding herself standing fully clothed in the shower, about to turn on the water, really shocked her into concentrating on what she was doing. Bitterly she reflected on what could happen to a girl when she allowed herself to be obsessed by a man who certainly wasn't worth the agony of unrequited love. She should have learnt from Tony. One lesson should have been enough!

Having managed to pull herself together sufficiently to take a normal shower, she reached in her wardrobe for a satin wrap and slid it on. She had bought it in Shrewsbury, with a few minutes she hadn't been able to fill. It was much too beautiful to wear casually round her small flat but she felt badly in need of something to cheer her up. She brushed her hair but used no make-up, having decided to have an early night. She saw a succession of such nights stretching before her, only remarkable for their sameness, and sighed.

Trailing to the kitchenette, she stuck a piece of lettuce between two slices of bread and carried it, with a large pot of coffee, back to her living room. She could pretend someone was coming to share the coffee, madness though it might be!

The doorbell rang and she went to answer it mechanically. She hadn't been here long enough to get to know many of her neighbours. It was probably the young couple in the downstairs flat wanting to borrow some sugar. They were always running out.

She was quite unprepared to find Lawton on the doorstep and failed to act quick enough to prevent him from stepping past her.

'I don't care for having doors slammed in my face,' he scowled, 'but you may close it now I'm inside.'

Neale was distractedly clutching together the two fronts of her négligé. The satin was slippery, making the sash difficult to tie securely.

'Bit late for that, isn't it?' Lawton mocked, letting his narrow-eyed glance scour over her discomfort.

'What do you want?' she whispered, seeing the answer in his eyes and hoping she wasn't reading correctly. If he wanted her where would she find the strength to resist him? Some mischief had brought him here, she sensed it. And being alone with him could spell disaster!

Her glance went anxiously over him. He was wearing jeans and they were tight. They clung to his powerfully shaped hips. A matching black body shirt replaced the collar and tie he normally wore for business, moulding the broad expanse of his shoulders and chest. He's flaunting his virility, like reinforcements for a battle, she thought. He knows exactly how sexy he is.

Aware how his nearness was driving the strength from her legs, she collapsed into a chair when she had been going to put on something more decorous. 'Please excuse me,' she said stiffly, 'I was just about to have,' she almost said dinner but as her glance fell on the wilting sandwich, she changed it hastily to, 'a snack.'

'Carry on,' he granted graciously, settling himself comfortably in the other chair. 'I'm glad you don't have a sofa, Neale.'

She was busy pouring a cup of coffee, intending offering it to him and getting another for herself. Her head came up with a jerk. 'Why?'

'A sofa often serves as a bridge to the bedroom,' he smiled cynically. 'Without one, only a man you really cared for would get as far as that.'

'I've never heard of anything so ridiculous!' she followed his reasoning exactly but choose to react with scorn. Almost throwing the coffee at him, she hurried to the kitchen for another cup, 'You still haven't told me what you're here for?'

His smile faded but there was nothing harsh in his face as he watched her sitting down again. Surprisingly he appeared to be choosing his words, as if he wanted to be sure he found the right ones. 'Did you think I would be content to leave things as they stood between us, this morning? The first minute I had, I had to find you, to take up where we left off.'

Neale swallowed, her fair head bowed to hide her sudden pain. 'Everything was settled. . . .'

'Far from it,' broodingly his glance wandered over her but the tenderness remained in his eyes. 'We left the Caribbean in a hurry, Neale, and I flew almost straight on to the Med. And since I returned on Thursday, I haven't known a moment's peace. If for some reason, you feel badly done by, how about me? Do you imagine that after spending two nights making love to the most delectable girl I've ever met, I can simply turn everything off? I'm urgently in need of you, Neale. You've become like a drug I can't do without.'

She recognised his addiction with an inner groan. It was a blissful high and if she kept on taking another dose she wouldn't be able to do without either. Shuddering, she clenched her hands, surprised to find they were damp with sweat. 'That's all you think about, isn't it? Sex?'

'Don't put words in my mouth, Neale,' he warned, his face hardening a little. 'I'm trying to be reasonable. I believe what we have going for us is worth fighting for but I don't want you frightened off before I start. There seems to be some confusion to unravel and because you're a woman you aren't going to help me. I have to guess. So—okay, fair enough. But if I'm forced to ask questions, you're going to have to oblige with a few answers.'

'No!' this hinted at exposure, something she wasn't prepared to face. Nor had she any wish to explain why she wouldn't become his mistress. If he wasn't sensitive enough to work it out for himself, she wasn't going to do it for him! 'I have nothing to add,' she said desperately. 'The Caribbean happened too suddenly, you rushed me off my feet. I've had time to reconsider and you're aware of my decision. No amount of talking's going to alter it.'

'Hush,' he smiled softly, as her voice came in little rushes, 'Don't panic. We'll work something out.'

To your advantage, I bet, she glared silently.

Pushing aside his coffee cup, Lawton suddenly rose and reached for her. She was jerked to her feet, right into his arms before she realised what he was doing. As her slight body sagged against him, her face coloured as she felt his instant reaction.

'You don't have to blush like a schoolgirl, Neale,' he said softly. 'You know how you effect me.'

'You're trying to trap me!' she gasped.

'Certainly not,' he said quite grimly, a faint frown creasing his forehead. 'I hate the word myself. Do what I want, my darling, and I'll give you the world but there won't be any strings. You'd be free to go whenever you wished.'

His voice was so softly seducing, she wondered what she was made of that she didn't give in. He even managed to give the impression that the outcome of his doubtful proposal was desperately important to him. She sighed, a muffled sound of half-smothered desire and Lawton used his own interpretation, his eyes beginning to glow softly as he anticipated her final capitulation.

Holding her slightly from him, he feasted his eyes on her astonishing young beauty. His gaze explored the delicate features of her face then went on to take in the rounded contours of her slender figure.

'Please!' Neale moaned as his expression darkened with passion and his head bent nearer, his intention obvious, as his glance homed in on her lips, 'Please stop and think.'

'God!' he muttered thickly. 'How can I, when you have me half out of my mind?'

Lifting her chin, he made her look at him though she could only do so for a few seconds. Her own mind was spinning and as his hands went over her, she could feel her heartbeats surging against his fingers, flowing from her body into his.

The blaze of his blue eyes scorched her like a fire as his mouth swiftly descended to smother her next protest with kisses. As his arms tightened she trembled with awareness as the warmth of his flesh seemed to sear her beneath the thin fabric of his vest. She was caught in a vortex she couldn't escape. She had to, but how could she when the feeling rushing through her rendered her powerless to move?

As the passion of exchanged kisses deepened, Neale's satin robe was roughly undone to allow Lawton's impatient hands ready access to her bare breasts. Groaning, he cupped their tautening fullness to his seeking lips, his tongue, in turn, greedily encircling each hardening nipple. Neale's breathing altered as a quickening stab of sensation lanced through her lower limbs, making her dizzy with longing for him.

His mouth, hot against her bare skin, was an enticement she couldn't resist. When his lips returned to hers, her slender arms encircled his neck, her fingers tracing a path over corded muscles.

'Darling, I need you,' he muttered hoarsely, picking her up and carrying her to the bedroom.

She lay on the bed, naked, entirely at his mercy. He leant over her, between kisses gently caressing every inch of her. She felt his hands moving heavily on her hips and waist then inexorably down her flat stomach. He was fully aroused, almost out of control, and not trying to hide it.

'These last five days have been like an eternity!' he muttered savagely. 'Now tell me you don't love me?'

The word love shocked her, even as she moaned and writhed against him. He hadn't raised his voice but she knew he was demanding that she should confess her feelings for him openly. The way he spoke revealed he would be satisfied with nothing less than her complete surrender. He wanted to hear her protesting her love for him until she hadn't a breath left in her body. But he didn't love her, and if she gave in to him he would force her to go to his apartment, where he would take everything she had to give until he was tired of her.

Aghast at her own folly, Neale rolled away from him, sudden terror giving her the strength to free herself. 'You're making a mistake!' she cried, everything blotted out but an animal instinct to survive. 'I hate you now, do you hear?' her voice rose hysterically, as if to make sure he did. 'I'll never forgive you. . . .'

The hot colour remained on his cheekbones but his eyes became as cold as ice. 'All right, Neale,' he cut in sharply. 'There's no need to shout, I heard you the first time and I've no wish to slap you. Not for telling me the truth, anyway.'

Stumbling to her feet, Neale groped blindly for her robe while he flung on his clothes. The harshness of his voice should have steadied her but she found she could scarcely stand. She was in such a state she didn't even know herself anymore. 'Lawton?' she gulped, her grey eyes enormous in her tortured face.

He held up a hand with no change of expression. 'You can spare me your excuses, you little fraud. I don't want to hear them. It's quite obvious you've had second thoughts and I don't intend to beg. Just be thankful I know when to give up—which is something a woman seldom learns!'

She heard the door slam like a clap of thunder in her ears, yet he had left fairly silently. With a feeling of irretrievable loss, she flung herself back on the bed, trying to gather a little warmth from the spot where his body had been. A part of her had died when he had closed the door and she felt she was bleeding. A wave of nausea surged in her throat as she wept silently into her pillow, knowing there was nothing now to soften the bleak desolation of the future.

The desolation persisted as autumn drew on towards winter and she submerged herself in work, but work didn't give her the same satisfaction any more and she often found it difficult to keep her mind on it. Weeks after he had walked out of her flat she kept on seeing the wintry look in Lawton's eyes, and, instead of fading, to her despair the image of his contempt grew daily more vivid. Could she have felt any worse, she wondered, if she had agreed to live with him?

The interior of the south coast hotel was coming along nicely. Rex was pleased with it, but the reponsibility for its completion rested entirely on Neale. He occasionally managed to get down to give his opinion but he was extra busy dashing backwards and forwards to Spain, supervising the team he had out there.

If Neale sometimes felt she was being rushed off her feet, she didn't complain. It was only when she was exhausted that she slept at nights without the aid of aspirin and hot milk. This morning she had motored to the hotel from London. In winter, having to travel round the country could be a bit of a bore, even an ordeal if the weather was particularly bad, but she preferred to come home at nights rather than sleep in a strange place.

Today the weather was foggy and raw. She slammed on the heater to discover it wasn't working, then her windscreen wipers packed in and she had to find a garage to fix them. It was probably going to be one of those days! she thought wryly.

It was. Throughout the day she was faced with a number of problems. Small ones, certainly, but enough to cause seething frustrations, especially when it was no fault of her own. Or so she thought!

She was staring with dismay at some mock-Tudor panelling which she had never authorised to be painted bright green, when Lawton arrived. She hadn't seen him since that last terrible evening. It was common knowledge that he had been out of the country but as she never so much as mentioned his name, if she could help it, she'd had no idea where. Seeing him now made her realise how much she had missed him. She felt his presence like the stimulation of strong wine. Everything changed, the air, the light, the sound of the sea, the cool tempo of her blood recharging to rushing warmth. Her eyes fixed on him hungrily and for the space of seconds she couldn't look away.

When she did catch his attention, he immediately strode over to where she was standing. 'Is everything going well, Miss Curtis?' he asked abruptly.

His use of her surname, the crispness of his voice, putting everything back to where it had been in the beginning, was like a death-knell. He didn't even look at her properly, seeming more interested in what was due to make him a lot of money.

'Good-afternoon, sir,' she murmured, unable to bring herself to say Mr Baillie, not when she had an insane desire to fling herself into his arms and whisper, 'my love!' 'Yes,' she tried to edge him away from the green panelling. 'Just one or two snags, here and there, sir, but nothing that can't be rectified.' Had he seen? She crossed tense fingers furtively.

'At my expense?'

As his brows rose cynically—those dear, dark brows her fingers ached to trace, she flushed. 'I—well, I suppose so, but there's always a contingency sum, you know.'

His eyes glittered derisively as they raked her flushed face. 'Don't presume to teach me my own business, Miss Curtis. From bitter experience I've learned that such allowances are rarely enough to cover the blunders of someone like yourself.' As Neale bit her lip in angry mortification, he snapped, 'Supposing you show me the worst that's happened today? I'm just in the mood to sort something out.'

Someone out, you mean? Neale thought silently, resignedly stepping aside so he could see the ruined panelling.

'My God!' he barked, 'Who on earth's responsible for this? It looks like an old-fashioned station waiting room!'

So far as she could remember they were usually dark brown but it sounded bad enough—it was bad enough! 'Someone obviously got mixed up, sir.'

He shot her a look of extreme irritation. 'This wasn't done today.'

'You could be right, sir. In ʻfact—No,' she agreed hurriedly, meeting his glacial glance.

'Why wasn't it checked before it reached this stage? If I'm not mistaken,' his eyes challenged her to say he was, 'that's the finishing coat.'

Her cheeks flushed again at the implication of negligence. 'The firm we employ for the specialised work always does a first-class job, Mr Baillie. They've never given us any cause to suspect anything like this might happen.'

'That doesn't answer my question,' he said grimly. 'You're merely offering an excuse for skipping proper supervision.'

'The—that's not fair!' Neale stammered, 'I can assure you. . . .'

Ruthlessly he cut in. 'Just let me say, Miss Curtis, if it happens again, it will be out of your pocket! I employ people to make money, not to squander it. If you're too lazy to check every inch of what's being done, then I suggest you're in the wrong job.'

The coldness of his voice shook her as much as what he said. He was right, of course. If she hadn't been so eager to wallow in self-pity these past weeks she might have noticed several things sooner. Yesterday, for instance, if she hadn't let herself be drawn nostalgically to the seashore, she would have had time to check these suites. She could indulge in one glorious moment of defiance, like telling Lawton to go take a jump from the top of the building, but where would that get her? He would have the last laugh when he sacked her—even quicker than he threatened to!

'I can always find another job, Mr Baillie.'

'Can you?'

After deciding not to defy him, she had been unable to restrain all her resentment. Now she regretted her own foolishness as ice glazed his eyes.

'You won't get a reference from me,' he added, his voice even colder than his expression.

She knew when she was beaten, she hadn't a chance. 'I can only repeat that I'm sorry, sir. . . .'

'I must have missed it the first time,' he retorted sarcastically.

'I'm sorry,' she muttered inanely, dropping her head to hide tears. God! he knew how to hurt but did he have to go on stabbing her? Her eyes stung but not half as badly as her feelings.

'You'd better lead on to the next little mistake,' he commanded, his tone ripping her to pieces.

She turned, stumbling. 'The wrong fitments in number 85,' she heard herself whispering, while wondering where her brains were? Why hadn't she kept quiet about that and shown him the wrong-coloured taps in one of the ground-floor powder rooms? That mightn't have infuriated him as much.

Like an old-fashioned taskmaster he followed, berating her as they proceeded, not caring who overheard. 'Were there no other applicants when Rex took you on? It seems we spend taxpayers' money educating a lot of idiots! We might have done better to have employed someone straight from kindergarten. I can't say I can commend such dedication to duty, Miss Curtis! You mess up your personal life, now you seem bent on transferring your incompetency to me!'

Neale stumbled again, so blinded by tears she failed to see where she was going. He was flaying her alive. He might as well have had a whip—it couldn't have hurt more!

Suddenly, as the floor level on the corridor dropped, Neale found herself flying. Her feet caught on a hose from a cleaning machine and she crashed headlong down a flight of steps.

Fortunately there were just four but, she landed in a heap at the bottom. Somewhere she hit her head and the world spun dizzily. She tried to jump up again but couldn't. Her legs wouldn't support her and with a helpless sob she slumped against the wall.

'Are you all right, darling?' a voice penetrated her dazed ears anxiously.

She couldn't have heard correctly but she nodded, as gentle arms gathered her up and she was carried into a bedroom.

'Damn,' she heard Lawton mutter, for no furniture had arrived yet and there wasn't even a chair. She struggled to open her eyes, to reassure him. 'There's nothing wrong with me, Lawton, except the shock of a little tumble. You can put me down.'

His mouth tightened as he lowered her to a sample of carpeting which had got left lying around. As his hands began going closely over her she began to think hazily that it must be worth nearly getting killed to be so close to him again.

'Nothing seems broken,' he breathed, 'but I'm going to get someone to confirm it. Don't you dare move.'

Most of the working teams had finished for the day but she heard him ordering someone outside to fetch the nurse. When he stepped back inside his face was full of concern and his voice so gentle he was just like the old Lawton she loved.

Her eyes filled with tears but she forced a faint smile. 'I should have been looking where I was going. It was my own fault.'

'It was mine,' he said tersely, kneeling beside her again and smoothing the tumbled hair from her brow with fingers she couldn't believe were shaking. 'You've quite a bump on your head. Oh, God, Neale, I'm sorry!'

'Once I get my breath back I'll be fine,' she stiffened against the inclination to cling to him. 'I don't want any fuss.'

The nurse from the company's medical unit interrupted what might have developed into another argument, and, after a few minutes, confirmed that Neale had no broken bones, but when Neale retorted, impatiently, that of course she hadn't, she was told, more severely, that she could have had, and that she would certainly have some bruises in the morning.

'You've been lucky, Miss Curtis,' Nurse Brown frowned. 'A fall of any kind can give you a nasty shock and that bump on your head could have been worse.'

Neale nodded contritely and submitted to having a piece of plaster stuck over a slight cut. What else could she do when it was so apparently two against one?

When the nurse had gone, she said wryly, 'I just hope my car will start.'

Lawton frowned. 'You can't drive tonight. You'd better come back with me.'

'I can't ruin both your business and your evening!' she protested, 'Lawton, that panelling . . .!'

'Forget it,' he said curtly, a look of frustration and remorse on his face, 'I don't know what came over me. What does it matter if it was painted red, white and blue! I had no call to rip into you like that.'

Neale drew a tremulous breath. That sounded like an apology but she couldn't be sure. He was probably only trying to make her feel better. She had been guilty of negligence and he was the boss. On the whole, she had maybe got off lightly.

She began walking to the door and he asked abruptly, 'Where do you think you're going?'

'If I'm getting a lift back to town,' she said, without turning, 'I'd better see to my car first.'

'That won't be necessary,' catching up with her, he held out his hand, 'Let me have your keys and I'll arrange for it to be delivered to your flat.'

It didn't take long to get back to London. Lawton didn't talk much but Neale was very conscious of him sitting beside her. The comfort of the luxurious Rolls he was driving was such that she ought to have been completely relaxed. Instead, she had to forcibly will herself into a deceptive calm.

Wearly she slumped in her seat. Her head ached slightly and she felt tired, at least two things that should have stopped her thoughts from straying in Lawton's direction. But he had been away almost a month and she hadn't realised how hungry she had been for the sight of him. And, if his anger had alarmed her, his gentleness afterwards made her even more apprehensive. Loving him so much made her too vulnerable. She wanted to fling her arms about his neck and whisper she would live with him or do whatever he liked. But she knew she dared not!

In London he parked outside her flat and insisted on

carrying her upstairs. Anticipating her protests before
she voiced them, he said, 'I think you need some hot,
sweet tea, Neale, and while you're drinking it I'm going
to cook you your dinner. This is no time to remember
how independent you have to be.'

Lowering her carefully into a chair, he murmured
gently, as if aware of the tenseness in her body, 'Relax,
I shan't be a minute.'

'I'd like a wash,' her tongue flicked her lips nervously
as she tried not to notice the look he bent on her. 'And,
unless you'd rather wait, I'm really quite capable of
making my own tea.'

'I'd rather wait,' he replied quietly. 'But don't be too
long or I'll have to come and see what you're doing.'

Neale washed quickly but didn't wear her satin robe.
Finding a thicker one, she huddled into it, grateful for
the extra warmth. Her movements disconcertingly
clumsy, she combed her hair, taking care not to catch
her bruised forehead. Any other bruises she had
wouldn't show but her face might look a mess in the
morning!

Lawton was waiting with the promised cup of tea,
along with one for himself. He'd placed them both on a
low table before the gas fire. There was no sign of
dinner and she didn't know whether to be regretful or
relieved that he could be leaving sooner than she had
thought.

The tea was nice though, and he had found her small
tin of biscuits, to which he helped himself idly. After
making sure she was comfortable, he stretched out his
long legs and gazed at the fire.

After five minutes had passed without a word being
exchanged and he seemed in danger of falling asleep,
she exclaimed indignantly. 'You can't be that tired!'

Opening his eyes, he contrived to look hurt. 'Making
your tea took a lot of effort.'

'Don't you mean your holiday has made you lazy?'
She wished she hadn't sounded so reproachful,

especially when he replied, sternly, 'I haven't been on holiday, Neale.'

She tried to make amends, for he was really being very kind. 'I'm sorry if I jumped to the wrong conclusions. You look tired and I—I think you have a few grey hairs, but you've also a wonderful tan. . . .'

He grinned, his glance teasing. 'I'm told that any grey hairs I possess are only visible if one looks very closely.'

This was so true that Neale flushed. What a fool she was, betraying herself so blatantly! 'I suppose you've been sorting out details for your island?' she mumbled hastily.

The gleam of near triumph died from his eyes to be replaced by one closer to resentment. 'I've lost interest in that. I might even resell it.'

So he hadn't been there. She sighed in somewhat weary perplexity. Wherever he had been he obviously had no wish to talk about it and she didn't wish to appear to be over-curious.

As she sighed, he glanced at her intently again. 'Is your head still aching?'

'No, I'm actually feeling much better,' in some ways, she amended silently, as having him so near without being able to touch him began tormenting her intolerably.

'Good,' he smiled, seemingly not noticing the state she was in.

She was trying to smile back when the doorbell rang. 'Sit still,' he commanded, at her side in an instant, his hand on her shoulder, holding her down as she began to get up, 'I'll go.'

While she tensed uncertainly, he went to see who was there and her eyes widened in bewilderment as it was obviously someone, by the way he spoke to them, whom he had been expecting.

'Welcome,' he was saying, adding wryly, 'I was beginning to think you'd got lost.'

Holding open the door, he ushered two women

carrying covered containers through to Neale's tiny kitchenette. 'Just put everything on the bench, Sara,' he instructed charmingly, as if this was something he did every day. 'We'll help ourselves.'

'Thank you, Mr Baillie,' Sara glanced at him, much too adoringly, Neale thought, as she did as she was told then disappeared again with her assistant, out into the night.

CHAPTER NINE

NEALE had scarcely got her breath back when the door closed. It was like being visited by someone from outer space! She stared at the smug expression on Lawton's face. 'How on earth did you arrange all this?'

'While you were changing I used your phone,' he explained, 'to contact the catering firm I sometimes use. And,' he executed a triumphant wave, kitchen-wards, 'behold—dinner!'

'You were going to cook it, I thought?' she accused.

'Haven't I done you enough injury for one night?' he asked sardonically.

'You make a good cup of tea. . . .'

'And I'm a fair hand at a barbecue,' he grinned, 'Where I can shove my mistakes discreetly in the fire, but I had no intention of lowering my prestige by serving you burned steaks.'

She couldn't imagine him doing anything less than well, but when she giggled and he raised dark brows in polite enquiry, she merely stopped laughing and said, 'I do appreciate the trouble you've gone to. It's certainly a pleasant surprise, but you must let me do my bit.'

She wanted to begin serving the meal but, again, he wouldn't let her get up. 'Stay where you are,' he said firmly. 'I also took advantage, in your absence, to set two trays. This won't take a minute.'

He hadn't overlooked a thing and the food was marvellous. A delicious hors d'œuvres, chicken, melting in the mouth, done in an appetising continental fashion, followed by a delectable cold sweet and coffee.

'I'll allow you to serve the coffee,' Lawton passed her the percolator which he had plugged in as they finished. 'If you can manage that, I'll be able to leave with comparative peace of mind, knowing you will be all right.'

'I've ate so much I couldn't be any other,' she said ruefully. 'I don't know how I'm going to repay you.'

'By coming to dine with me, one evening,' he smiled.

Neale laughed, but her eyes misted. It was a wonderful game—of pretence! This was how it could be. Every evening she could play at keeping house, but that was all it would amount to. A lack of commitment would have its own careless delights. She might know the pleasures and none of the trauma of being a wife. She need never know what it was to worry over a husband and children—unless one was stupid enough to want that kind of thing!

As a fierce longing for exactly such things whitened her face, Lawton sprang to his feet. 'You've had about enough for one night. And I don't mean food.'

As she raised startled eyes to his face, he swept the remains of their feast into a large plastic bag. 'See what a useful man I'd be to have around the house?' he quipped. 'I'll drop this in your dustbin on my way out.'

'You're going?'

'Yes,' the humour died from his eyes as he stared at her broodingly. 'You're looking far too tired. Take a day off and I'll look in again, some time tomorrow. Goodnight, Neale.'

He was gone, before the protest she was about to utter escaped her lips. Convulsively she clenched her hands in an effort to keep her mind off the past hours. It was better not to think of them, otherwise she might be tempted to take a course that was decidedly not for her!

Disregarding Lawton's advice, which she was sure he hadn't meant her to take seriously, she went to the office as usual the following morning. Her car was parked outside, as Lawton had promised it would be, but she had left it and taken the tube. She ought to go back to the hotel, but, at a pinch, she could probably manage to supervise by phone, for once? The small accident she had suffered hadn't left any serious repercussions but she didn't feel like facing the long drive to the coast.

She saw nothing of Lawton all day, though everywhere was humming with the news that he was back. On hearing he was in conference, and aware how this could lead to a dinner engagement, she was surprised to find him on her doorstep at eight o'clock.

Having felt tired, she hadn't bothered to do anything but shower and put on her warm robe. Now she was embarrassed that he must suspect she wore nothing else when she was at home. He made no remark about it, however, and she tentatively asked him to come in.

Not moving instantly, he stood watching her, the set of his head proud, his mouth firm. Neale tried not to get too absorbed in the hard masculine lines of his face. It was the dangerous way her heart started beating that warned her against letting down her guard.

Misreading her flicker of agitation, he frowned. 'You don't look very pleased to see me. Were you expecting someone else?'

'I heard you were busy,' she said shortly, not liking his inference that she had dressed this way for another man.

'I have been busy!' Suddenly he swept her inside, and, as he closed the door, bent and kissed her cheek. 'But I told you I would call.'

With every nerve in her body tingling, she shuddered. When would she learn not to judge him by other men! Yet in some ways wasn't he the same? He only wanted her for one thing; hadn't he made that plain? All the same, when he asked, with deep concern in his blue eyes, why she had come to work that day, she felt ashamed.

'How did you know?' she frowned.

'I learned,' he retorted menacingly, 'If I hadn't been in the middle of a board meeting at the time, I would have come down. Actually it wasn't that which stopped me,' his mouth quirked with faint amusement. 'Knowing you, I anticipated the argument that would ensue if I ordered you home—and that I hadn't time for.'

She shivered as his glance moved intently over her, as he suddenly stopped hiding a need to look at her closely. Neale gripped her arms tightly behind her back, in order to prevent them reaching out to him. To hide the depth of feeling surging through her, she forced a casual smile. 'Well, it was nice of you to call, but I really am fine. I won't keep you.'

'In a great hurry to get rid of me, aren't you?' he jeered, 'I wonder why?'

How could she confess that because of the yearning eating away inside her, she couldn't trust herself with him! 'I thought you might be tied up this evening, too,' she said lamely.

'So you have made other arrangements!'

'No!' her voice rose as he seemed to be deliberately picking her up the wrong way. 'I meant as well as your being busy this afternoon, I wasn't referring to myself.'

His eyes narrowed but he suddenly raked a large hand through his dark hair. 'Oh, damn!' he said softly, 'I didn't come here tonight to upset you. How about a cup of coffee? I guess I could do with one.'

'Yes, of course,' far too eager to please him, she fled to the kitchenette.

He followed, filling the small space completely, overpowering her with his sheer size. 'There isn't room for both of us,' she objected, feeling her pulse begin to pound.

'I'll take my jacket off, shall I?' he teased, proceeding to do so while he watched her face. As his coat dropped over a chair, he asked innocently, 'Is this better? Can you breathe?'

'No!' Neale gasped helplessly as he drew her gently into his arms. She felt his body against hers and she

seemed to melt as his hand trailed along the rounded
side of her breast down to her waist. Her heart leapt as
he breathed her name and his hard lips covered her own
with a hungry, compelling swiftness. Neale moaned
softly as something leapt instantly to life inside her,
kindling fires that warmed and weakened her lower
limps. His every touch scorched her skin and her
powers of resistance were nil.

It wasn't until she became aware of the throbbing
hardness of his body that she took fright. Tensing, she
tugged at his hands, trying to free herself as conflicting
emotions tore through her. The nearly overwhelming
physical and emotional need she felt to surrender
completely made her realise how little time she had if
she had any hope of escaping him.

'Lawton, please!' she murmured tremulously.

Gently he brushed the tousled hair from off her hot
forehead, his eyes shuttered yet searching. 'I'm not
thinking in terms of assault, darling. I would never
hurt you.'

How could he help it! 'The coffee,' she whispered
tonelessly.

He waited until the pulse in her throat stopped
pounding then tenderly let her go. 'Do we have cups or
mugs?' he asked, surveying her small display of both.

'Mugs,' she replied numbly. He had kissed her as
though he could have devoured her, as if he had been
starved for the feel and taste of her. In another
moment, she suspected they both knew, there would
have been no drawing back.

He passed her two mugs and reached for a tray as she
began filling them. She had to get rid of him before he
touched her again. Somehow she had to find the
strength!

He carried the tray and she followed, too conscious
of his long muscled back and powerful thighs. Why
didn't she just ask him to go? Weeks ago, when he had
been here, before he left he had said he had no wish to

see her again, so what was preventing her reminding him of that! She took a gulp of the coffee he passed her then put it down abruptly. He was! She had to face the truth. She loved him so much that even just being able to look at him was a something she couldn't easily forgo.

'You were away a long time?' she had to lower her eyes to the carpet to hide the agony of despair in them.

'Missed me?' he leaned forward, his voice husky.

'Yes,' she admitted weakly.

'You don't have to miss me, you know,' he put his mug aside to come over and hunker down beside her. 'We have so much going for us, Neale.' Rocking slightly forward, his hands gripped her waist, thumbs pressing upwards, dark eyes burning into her. 'God, Neale! do I have to spell out exactly how I feel?'

Just as she was about to respond to an instinctive blind hunger, the doorbell rang. With a single reflex action and an exclamation of disgust, Lawton was on his feet. 'It's after nine. Do you often have visitors this late?' he rasped.

He made nine o'clock sound like the middle of the night and before she could protest he was pulling the door open. To her amazement it was Tony!

As she gasped his name, it must have dawned on Lawton that this was her ex-fiancé, for his mouth tightened. 'Yes, what do you want?' he barked grimly.

Glancing furtively at Lawton's thunderous face, Tony gulped hastily at Neale, 'You asked me to call.'

'I—did?' she frowned, briefly disconcerted.

Tony took immediate advantage of her confusion. 'Of course you did, darling. Don't you remember——'

She couldn't, and was aware of nothing but the icy contempt in Lawton's eyes. 'I must have forgotten,' she said numbly.

'Don't mind me,' Lawton said curtly, retrieving his jacket, 'I'm late for an appointment as it is.'

As the sound of his forbidding footsteps receded down the stairs, Neale came slowly out of her frozen trance. 'I'm not asking you in,' she snapped at her ex-fiancé, 'I don't believe I ever asked you to call in the first place!'

'You didn't,' he confessed unhappily, 'but that. man looked positively dangerous. I had to say something!'

Neale's bewilderment increased. 'I wasn't aware you even knew my address.'

'I didn't,' his voice held a slight swagger, 'I'm travelling a lot for the firm these days, you know, and I met your parents in Australia. They gave it to me.'

'They had no business!' she cried, slightly stunned.

'I'm getting a divorce, Neale!' he exclaimed. 'When I said I had made a mistake and would like another chance with you, they gave me their blessings and told me where you lived.'

It was a relief that she could still look into Tony's handsome face without a twinge of desire or regret for anything but the years she had perhaps foolishly wasted. Seeing him tonight merely confirmed what she had learned weeks ago. 'I'm afraid you've all been wasting your time,' she replied coldly. 'I've discovered there's nothing so dead as dead love—if,' she added, 'it was ever that with us, in the first place. I'd advise you, Tony,' she sighed wearily, 'to go back to your wife.'

After Tony left, she returned to her chair in a dream. She tried to concentrate on remembering her parents but she hadn't heard from them for three months and their images kept fading. She should at least have asked how they were but she had no awareness of anyone but Lawton. She could still smell the spicy scent of his aftershave, still see the tenderness in his eyes, still feel the seductive warmth of his mouth as he had kissed her. Her whole being burned for him, yet what was the use? Apart from the fact that he just wished to live with her, he had seen Tony and believed she had asked him here this evening. There had been contempt and disgust in his eyes and she didn't think she would have to worry again about keeping him at a distance.

Rex's good mood, next morning, contrasted so markedly with her bad one that it took Neale all her time not to glare at him. It hadn't taken many minutes to get rid of Tony but removing Lawton from her thoughts had been another thing altogether. His anger as he had left the flat haunted her, making sleep impossible, a fact betrayed by the paleness of her face as she walked into Rex's office.

'And you're to make sure you get there!' he was saying.

He had started talking as soon as she was through the door but she hadn't heard a word. 'I'm sorry,' she looked at him in dismay. 'I was miles away.'

Rex frowned impatiently. 'What you get up to at night is your own business but I'd appreciate it if you'd keep your mind on your work while you're here.'

'I'm sorry,' to her horror her voice wobbled. She was feeling dreadfully tense and it wasn't often Rex spoke to her sharply but she deserved his sarcasm.

'Never mind!' he said testily, giving her a sharp glance, 'I'm talking about the Christmas party, the one Mr Baillie gives in his own apartment. You have to attend.'

Neale gazed at him in consternation. 'I—I usually go to the big one. . . .'

Rex snorted. 'That's for all the firm and he rarely shows face. This other is different. It's for the heads of the departments and their immediate assistants. It would be impossible to get us all in, big though his apartment is. As well, he usually asks a few friends but it's mainly his managerial staff.'

'I think I'd rather not bother,' Neale faltered. Lawton wouldn't want her there anyway.

Looking not a little scandalised, Rex exclaimed. 'It's not so much an invitation as a royal command, girl. Mrs Talbot always went, so, unless you are ill—and I don't mean pretending to be—I won't accept any excuses!'

Neale was certain he would if she could have explained the situation between Lawton and herself to him, but how could she? She wished with all her heart Rex hadn't told her about the party until the day before. Constantly having to set the temptation of seeing Lawton against the agony of seeing him threatened to tear her in two. She did her work automatically, praying that something would guard her from making more mistakes while her mind was so dulled by unhappiness. She lay awake at nights trying to reconcile herself to a loveless future and lost count of the times she cried herself to sleep. The morning she saw Lawton's photo in one of the popular dailies with a beautiful model, she thought her unhappiness must have reached its peak!

A few days before the party, June rang her at work, inviting her to lunch. Oddly reluctant, she agreed to meet her at a quiet restaurant where June said they could talk. Neale almost refused, thinking it might be wiser, but June had been so nice to her on the yacht, she couldn't bring herself to disappoint her.

'It's good to see you again,' June beamed, as they sat down to eat. 'I've been meaning to get in touch ever since Freddy and I returned from the Caribbean with Lawton, but somehow there hasn't been time. Anyway, it's lovely to see you today.'

Neale looked uneasily down at her soup. June was so pleasant and friendly. She seemed happier than she had been the last time Neale had seen her and she had no wish to do anything that might bring even one shadow back to the other girl's face, yet their friendship couldn't continue, not as things stood. If she was to see June and Freddy, even occasionally, there might be a danger of bumping into Lawton, and the less she had to remind her of him the better. The way she felt, she couldn't bear to hear June even mentioning him, as she was doing now.

'You're looking well,' Neale glanced up again with a

forced smile, 'Cruising in the West Indies seems to have done you a lot of good.'

'It wasn't just the Caribbean,' to Neale's surprise, June blushed shyly. 'It was Freddy. Suddenly he began to change. To begin with I thought it was the baby, and it was. Only,' she hesitated radiantly, 'he eventually confessed how one day, when I wasn't feeling so good, he began wondering how he would feel if things went really wrong and he lost me? Oh, Neale!' she smiled softly, 'he said he felt like he had been hit with something really hard, and it was then that he realised how much I meant to him.'

'I'm so glad,' Neale whispered, her own eyes misting over like June's.

'I think we both suddenly grew up,' June sighed ruefully, 'I think we'd both been looking for the kind of perfection that's impossible to find, taking into account human frailty. Anyway, everything's a lot better between us now, and, somehow, I feel much more confident about the future.'

'I'm so glad,' Neale said again, really meaning it. People like June deserved to be happy. She just hoped Freddy would never let her down again.

'And how about you?' June asked, a keener note in her voice. 'I can't say you're looking any happier than Lawton. What happened after you left the yacht, Neale? I honestly believed you and he were in love.'

Her cheeks going cold, Neale tried to laugh lightly. 'You know how it is, June. Everyone falls in love in that kind of situation. That's where our cool English climate proves a blessing in disguise. It soon brings one back to one's senses.'

June frowned. 'I'm not convinced it was just moonlight and the southern hemisphere with Lawton, Neale. When he returned to the yacht, he was a changed man. There were days when we couldn't get a civil word out of him.'

'He had a lot on his mind, trouble on the continent, for one thing,' Neale said quickly.

'Neale!' June exclaimed patiently, 'Lawton has been dealing with trouble since you were probably still in your pram. No, I think his present mood has something to do with you.'

It was possible, Neale admitted silently. Lawton might have been disappointed that she wouldn't live with him but it was more likely to have its roots in other causes. 'He appears to be enjoying himself well enough with Nina York!' she retorted tartly. 'If he has been depressed he seems to have got over it.'

'You could be right.' June stared at her uncertainly, 'But it could be a case of frustration? Lawton's taken so many girls like Nina out, without them meaning a thing. I thought you were going to be different.'

Neale had to ask quickly, before pain overwhelmed her. 'Are you going to this party he's giving on Tuesday?'

'Yes,' June frowned faintly as Neale changed the subject abruptly, but apparently decided not to pursue it. 'I hoped you'd be coming, too. It's one of the things I wanted to speak to you about.'

Why she allowed June to talk her into promising to go to the party, Neale was never sure. Despite Rex's threats, right up to the last moment she had vowed she wouldn't be there, even if it meant having a slight collision with a bus! She supposed she had really given in to June's pleading because, deep inside her, she still couldn't resist an opportunity of seeing Lawton.

Despairing of such a weakness in her character, that wouldn't let her say no to temptation, she took a firm stand with herself over the matter of a new dress. She forced herself to be content with her oldest one which hadn't had an airing for three years. If she happened to meet Lawton at his party, she didn't want him to think she was trying to entice him further by wearing something more up-to-date and glamorous.

She was discouraged to see, on the night of the party, how her old black dress still suited her fantastically.

After brushing her hair to a gleaming cloud and making up her face, Neale gazed at her reflection in dismay, unable to believe the slender, beautiful looking girl was herself. The dress accentuated her every curve yet billowed in all the right places. Even the narrow-heeled, single-strapped sandals on her small feet managed to look incredibly seductive! Panic stricken, she was about to fling everything off again when she remembered the taxi, at the door, waiting, and that, if she didn't go soon, Rex might be on the phone any minute, demanding to know where she was? He had viewed her refusal to allow him to pick her up with deep suspicion. She was sure if it hadn't been for giving his wife the wrong impression, he would have come and dragged her to the party willy-nilly!

As she approached the door of Lawton's apartment, she thought of the few times she had been here before and realised she had never felt other than apprehensive. If only, she found herself hoping hollowly, this evening might have a happier outcome than the other two!

It was with some relief that she saw the penthouse was crowded, people were everywhere. Usually Neale didn't care for gatherings as crowded as this, but for once she was grateful, as she slipped unnoticed into the reception area. She had seen nothing of Lawton, nor did she wish to. If she could find a quiet corner and manage to remain hidden for an hour, then surely Rex would be satisfied and let her go home?

Edging her way, she believed unobtrusively, through the huge lounge where there was dancing, she almost gasped with dismay when Lawton found her.

He pounced immediately. 'Dance with me,' he smiled, pulling her towards him, as though the last time he had seen her he had been her friend and not her enemy.

Involuntarily her eyes jerked to his face, as she tried desperately to free herself and control her racing pulse. Meeting the cool challenge in his eyes, her heart sank. Through the painful excitement his closeness provoked, she was aware of intense danger. He possessed an unrestrained maleness which played havoc with her feverish senses.

The leap of fire within her brought an almost frenzied attempt to resist him. 'I'd rather have a drink.'

He appeared to be considering her request, and while he did so, she was subjected to a scrutiny which was nothing less than outrageous. His gaze lingered for a few moments on eyes that were wide with distress despite all efforts to keep them cold and blank, then wandered on to taut breasts and the over-rapid beat of her heart between them.

'I'd like a drink,' she repeated, frantic to achieve some state of normality. She knew clearly that she would never manage this if he forced her to dance with him. Even having him looking at her was more than she could endure calmly.

'Later,' he laughed, his arms going round her relentlessly. 'Having just found you, I'm not giving you a chance to disappear.'

Wasn't his model here? Neale tried to fix her mind on this other girl as she was drawn tightly against Lawton's powerful body, but dominating all else was the impression of virility he exuded. His compelling sexual appeal left Neale weak when she wanted to be strong! Lawton Baillie must be every girl's dream of what a real man must look like but, she told herself frantically, he wasn't for her.

He pulled her closer, bending his lips to her ear. 'You're very beautiful, this evening,' he murmured huskily, as they circled the floor. 'I've been desperate to have you in my arms again.'

'I—I nearly didn't come,' she couldn't allow herself to be seduced with such talk!

'I threatened Rex with instant dismissal if you didn't. You probably saved his career.'

So that was why poor Rex had been in such a panic. 'He did his best,' she retorted angrily, 'but I wish you hadn't said anything. Heaven knows what he's been thinking.'

'I dream of the day when you need no persuading to be with me,' Lawton said thickly. 'When I see you standing on my doorstep, without an invitation, I'll know you've given in.'

'Never!' she gasped as the heat in his words exploded the kind of hunger inside her she was striving to ignore.

'Never is a long time!' he muttered softly, 'I've never been known to give up.'

She tried to hold herself passive and unprotesting but was too aware of the fierceness of the emotions running between them. Her anger faded and she knew a terrible grief that the situation between them couldn't have been different. Lawton wanted her and she wanted him, but while her needs were solely confined to one man, he played around with other women. He wanted them to live together but was making it very clear that, as well as having no intention of marrying her, he was also unwilling to give up any of his little diversions!

This thought led naturally to another, equally depressing. 'I saw you in the newspapers,' she murmured miserably.

'Did you?' he grimaced indifferently, 'The media are everywhere, one rarely escapes them.'

Rawly it came out. 'You were with Nina York.'

'Ah ...' he paused, with a noticeable hint of satisfaction, 'Were you jealous?'

'Of course not!' she retorted, too shrilly.

'I hoped you might be,' he said softly.

'I'm sure that wouldn't be the main point of the exercise!' she taunted. 'And I think you have a nerve pretending an interest in me when you're dining every evening with other girls!'

From the movement of his mouth against her hair, she knew he was grinning. Incensed she added icily, 'You have a distorted sense of humour!'

'If I didn't hang onto it, where the hell would I be?' his tone changed. 'You know what you do to me.'

Feeling the hardness of his body against her, she flushed and he said thickly, 'Oh, Neale, darling . . .'

It was then that a light voice interrupted them. 'May I cut in, please?'

Lawton paused, slowly relaxing his tight hold of the girl in his arms, his eyes moving enigmatically to the tall, glamorous brunette standing beside him. 'Nina?'

'I thought you'd be surprised, darling,' she laughed. 'You know how I adore parties—and when you mentioned this one. . . .'

Neale swallowed, feeling she had hit the very depth of humiliation. How dared Lawton play such games? Or was he just trying to crucify her? Her face pale, she turned away. 'Excuse me,' she murmured.

She saw June and hurried over to her. 'I was looking for you,' June smiled and began introducing her to the group of friends she and Freddy were busy talking to. Some Neale vaguely remembered meeting the first time she had been here but others were strangers.

June drew her aside. 'We were just about to tackle the buffet,' she murmured. 'Would you like to join us or are you having supper with Lawton?'

'No,' Neale confessed, unable to hide her despondency, 'Nina York has arrived and she seems the kind of girl who needs all his attention.'

'Nina York?' June looked puzzled, 'Are you sure?'

'I've just been talking to them.'

June glanced at Neale's white face and frowned. 'I could have sworn,' she began, then broke off abruptly, 'Oh, well, never mind. I suppose Lawton knows what he's doing and I think you could do with a drink!'

Neale was about to refuse when she suddenly caught a glimpse of Nina and Lawton dancing together and June's suggestion proved the perfect excuse to escape from the lounge and not have to watch them. Trying to pretend that a drink was exactly what she wanted, she followed June and Freddy to the dining room.

Rex was there with some people from the office and she noticed the relief on his face when he saw her. She waved to him and his wife and was rewarded with a beam of approval.

The buffet was delicious, with everything imaginable to eat and drink. Neale wasn't hungry but after two cups of coffee she felt better and a glass of white wine gave her sufficient courage to dance with a friend of the Fieldings when they returned to the lounge. Unfortunately the young man kept trying to kiss her. He wasn't drunk but he had been imbibing too freely, something Neale wished ruefully she had noticed sooner. He began to remind her of some of the men she had met in the Caribbean.

She felt even worse when she saw Lawton watching her, a contemptuous expression in his eyes. She wondered why she didn't look at him the same way. Instead she contented herself with smiling as pleasantly as she could up at her partner, trying to hide her aching heart. Lawton liked his own freedom but was apparently not keen that others should share the same privilege!

While his grim stare scorched her, she believed he would keep his distance. She was stunned when he pushed through the crowd and parted her almost roughly from the man she was dancing with. 'My dance, I think?' he said suavely.

As the young man protested, Lawton whirled her away. Neale had prayed to be rescued but now, perversely, she felt furious. 'There was no need for that!' she exclaimed, 'Timothy's very nice—June introduced us.'

'Remind me to strangle her some time,' he retorted coldly. 'Timothy's all right but he's no use to anyone in his present state.'

'I was only dancing with him!' she glared, 'You didn't have to be so abusive.'

He said reproachfully, 'You didn't seem to mind when someone cut in before.'

He was jumping to the wrong conclusions! 'You mean when Miss York grabbed you?'

'How delicately you put it,' he grinned.

Like a small chick, Neale's feathers ruffled. 'What have you done with her?'

Again he smiled, 'Introduced her to someone else. I believe they have already departed.'

Neale frowned doubtfully. Lawton sounded too glib. 'Did she go willingly?'

'My friend has great powers of persuasion. Something,' he added meaningly, 'I occasionally envy him.'

'All the same. . . .'

'Neale, darling,' he groaned, 'you're wearing yourself out worrying over things that needn't concern you. Why not relax?'

His arms caught her tighter and somehow the faint voice that insisted she must resist was silenced. She found herself moving in a dream, her protests unuttered. Fire, born of the wine, the music and Lawton's nearness began to run along her veins. The hand she raised involuntarily to push him away lifted instead to rest lightly on his shoulders.

They swayed to the music, barely moving, and she recalled dazedly another time they had danced like this. She could hear his breathing deepen and the desire she fought so much to hide swept through her, making it a nonsense for her to deny their mutual need.

Lawton's hands stroked restlessly on her back. 'We move so well together, Neale. Do you remember the first time we made love? You were like an extension, a part of me. I hadn't known two people could become one so completely.'

'Please!' she whispered, senses reeling. 'Someone might hear!'

'What of it?' he murmured huskily, 'You understand what I'm talking about.'

She did, only too well, and it showed. Showed in the way her hands twined convulsively round his neck and her body melted to the warm, hard strength of his. She trembled as his lips touched her throat, sending a hot urgency shooting through her. Her eyes fluttered and closed as the music swelled and she moved her head slightly until his seeking mouth found hers.

His kiss might only have been brief but she was swaying and disoriented when the band stopped playing and he let her go. There was a mist before her eyes, as though he had woven a spell about her, and for a moment she couldn't see.

Then, as her vision cleared and Lawton spoke to someone who approached him, Neale made her way to the cloakroom where she had left her coat. She moved automatically, she couldn't think straight, all she knew was she had to get home. Somehow Lawton was aware of her feelings, which would give him more power over her than he had already, and he might not hesitate to use it! She had given in to him once but the principles she had adhered to all her life were still the ones she must live by. One mistake might be excused but she could never forgive herself two!

She was on her way out when Lawton found her. Angrily he exclaimed. 'Just where do you think you're going to, Neale?'

Blindly she shook her head. Had he no mercy? He moved so silently, like a huge cat. She hadn't heard him coming.

There were people about but he took no notice of them. 'Come with me,' he took her arm, the apparent lightness of his grip belied by steely fingers.

'Lawton!' she breathed, her eyes wide and steady despite the way her heart was beating. 'I don't believe we have anything more to say to each other.'

Ignoring her feeble attempt to escape him, he urged her towards the library, through the door which he locked behind him. 'I want to talk to you,' he said firmly. 'And I'm not risking being interrupted. How quickly you get out of here depends entirely on how sensible you're prepared to be.'

CHAPTER TEN

NEALE found it very hard to maintain her composure. He was no more than inches from her and despite her decision to have nothing more to do with him, she was overwhelmed by a desire to be cradled in his arms. It took every bit of control she possessed not to throw herself at him, as her resolution wavered.

Unevenly she said, 'I don't want to stay, especially not here!'

A muscle tightened in his jaw. 'My bedroom's the only other place we can be alone.'

'Won't people be wondering where you are?' her face was cold and she knew she was practically gabbling, but the urge to touch him was growing so rapidly she wasn't sure how long she could resist it.

To her dismay he lifted her chin and looked straight into her eyes. 'They're enjoying themselves out there. They don't need us, or, more correctly, we don't need them. All I'm conscious of is the need we have for each other. And don't pretend you haven't felt it, my darling. You can be very responsive when you forget all your little inhibitions, and very passionate.'

The darkness of his pupils told her he hadn't forgotten, he remembered each detail of those nights in the Caribbean as clearly as she did. 'Do you have to be so cruel?' she asked unsteadily.

As she moistened dry lips, he must have guessed her fears for he relented a little. 'I won't force myself on you, Neale. Not that I would have to do that to get a response but I'd rather you came to me of your own free will.'

The air between them was thick with tension more intense than anything she had ever experienced. Lawton was holding back but the glint in his eye was dangerous.

'You ask the impossible!' she gasped.

'Yes,' he acknowledged bitterly. 'Maybe I do. You were probably born with a rigid code of conduct nothing to do with Tony. I blew my chances, didn't I, when I couldn't wait? I thought you were experienced and when I discovered you weren't I ploughed straight on, outraging your maidenish virtue.'

Stung, she retorted, 'You know that's not—well, completely true.'

'The qualification is useless, Neale,' he said grimly, 'unless you're prepared to tell me what went wrong?'

She swallowed painfully. 'You tried to trap me into a relationship I—I wasn't ready for.'

'Are you yet?' he laughed scornfully. 'Just how ready do you have to be? You could satisfy me a thousand times over and I'd still be back for more. And if that shocks your delicate sensibilities, I don't apologise. When we made love I thought I'd found everything I hadn't believed existed outside fairy tales and I honestly don't know what went wrong.'

If he didn't know she certainly wasn't going to tell him! But she had to be careful when, far from shocking her, his vibrant words sent waves of excitement cascading through her bloodstream. 'Life has to be more than sex,' she murmured bleakly. 'We don't even think the same way.'

'I'm sure that's not true,' his eyes were narrowed and watchful. 'Sex would be very important to us but I'm not fool enough to imagine it's the whole thing. If it would help, I would promise not to be too demanding, at least not at first.'

A shudder went through her and she caught her breath. If they were together she wouldn't mind what he demanded. Didn't he know how she dreamt continually of being in his arms, of belonging to him again, of having her dreams turned into total reality? For a moment she went quite limp, then she stiffened. 'Rex said you're probably going away again soon.

When you come back you'll have forgotten all about me.'

'Is that what you want?'

She tried to say yes but couldn't. 'I want what's best for you,' she replied bleakly.

He watched her closely. 'I'll be gone three weeks, Neale. In Greece, this time.'

She would miss him, it couldn't be otherwise, but one got used to everything, even pain. She forced a smile of deceiving brightness. 'Another hotel?'

'There's something I'm interested in and I'm combining other business. I have a certain amount of shipping.'

'Don't your employees qualify for free cruises?' she quipped.

'A lifetime of free cruises,' he murmured, following as she moved restlessly across the room. 'For a certain employee, if she so wishes.'

Neale tensed as he turned her to him again. 'I can't believe you would ask no payment.'

Curving both hands on her cheeks, he seemed to sense she was no longer teasing. 'If payment was asked, would it be so terrible?'

Stirring feverishly beneath the intensity of his gaze, she was at loss for words.

'Don't you remember St Lucia?' he insisted, watching the colour come and go in her face.

'I'm trying to forget!'

'I can't,' he said hoarsely. 'And I don't think you can either. Yet when I ask you to live with me you refuse.'

'I have to!' she whispered, closing her eyes.

His breath played on her closed lids. 'Don't you want me to make love to you, Neale? How can you say no when I can feel everything about you burning up for me?' Astutely he placed a hand on her throbbing heart. 'Your heart speaks for itself. Whatever your mind says, your body betrays you.'

'No!' she cried.

'Yes,' his voice was inexorable as he drew her against him, his arms tightening below her waist to lift her on her toes so she could feel his desire matching her own. Her lashes fluttered then fell as she saw the sensual curve of his mouth drawing nearer then felt it crushing her own passionately. Desire shot through Neale like a flame and she responded helplessly, like a small cat to the sun as his lips plundered and his hands caressed her, their deepening kisses betraying a ravenous hunger not to be appeased by mere touching.

'Darling!' Lawton muttered hoarsely, lifting his mouth for a second, as though sensing from the way she was clinging to him, how close she was to giving in, 'I want you.'

He only allowed her one breath before his head descended again to plant a trail of more gentle kisses over the rest of her face. It was his tenderness that proved her undoing. With a sigh she suddenly surrendered, having no more strength for such an unequal struggle. A savage flame consumed her as she began returning his caresses with a passion matching his. There was a burning sensation in her eyes and throat as Lawton's lips moved urgently over them as he picked her up and carried her to the sofa.

Laying her on it almost reverently, he threw off his jacket and stretched out beside her. 'You want me too, don't you?' he blazed.

His eyes glowed like the fire in his words and there was nothing she could do but say yes.

'I have to have you!' he said huskily, 'I can't wait another minute.'

She shivered as his mouth began a nerve-tingling assault once more while his hands slipped the narrow straps of her dress from her shoulders, baring her full curves to his worshipping gaze. As he caressed the creamy skin, she ran her palms over the hard muscles of his back, the need to touch him an unslakeable thirst. She had waited so long for this moment, never expecting it to come again and felt slightly intoxicated that it had. A soft moan escaped her as her fingers knotted themselves convulsively in his thick, dark hair.

He was drinking in her sweetness like a man parched in the desert and she was aware of the depth of desire revealed by his hardening thighs, yet some small measure of reserve remained. As a murmur of voices outside reached them, she choked, 'We can't, not here!'

'The door's locked,' he said thickly.

'Please?' she pleaded.

Looking into her anxious eyes, he saw how worried she was. 'Later then,' he relented.

She nodded, too abandoned to be able to concentrate on anything but complete reunion with him. He began a slow exploration of her mouth and when his hands returned to her breasts and the pink nipples hardened to his sensuous teasing, she was lost. 'How can I wait?' he groaned, his body full of masculine aggression.

Neale twisted from under him, her cheeks hot. 'We must,' she gasped.

He sighed gently. 'If I have to be patient, you'll have to help me, but I warn you I won't be so easily diverted in Greece.'

A frown touched her smooth brow. 'You're expecting me to go with you?'

'Naturally,' he smiled, swinging his feet to the floor but pulling her up beside him, keeping his arms round her as he ruefully adjusted her dress. 'You're so beautiful, my darling, I can't do without you.'

'But Lawton,' she glanced at him nervously, 'what would I do all day? You'll be busy.'

'There will be the evenings,' he said happily. 'And I won't be working all the time. I can promise,' he added with a teasing smile, 'you won't be bored.'

That wasn't what she meant but she let it pass. 'The real snag is,' she said slowly, 'that it might be impossible for me to take a holiday just now. I'm right in the middle of the south coast job, as you know, and Rex is tied up in Spain.'

'Someone else can do your work,' he retorted firmly, 'There must be someone capable of taking over?'

'Oh, but. . . .'

'Neale!' he broke in adamantly. 'For once in your life, my child, you are going to abandon everything. The old Neale has gone, remember.'

'I'd rather not give my job up though,' she protested.

'I don't see how you can keep it,' he replied, but speaking lightly, as if he wasn't prepared to make an issue of it. 'You won't need to work, you know.'

She would when he didn't want her any more. When he tired of her she would need a job very badly. He might insist on settling some money on her but her pride would never allow her to accept it. In taking her chance of happiness, she wasn't foolish enough to ignore the future. It was imperative that she retained some independence to enable her to survive the devastation that would occur after they parted.

'There's my flat,' she went on, deciding to disregard what he said about her not working, 'It's not a good time of year to close it up.'

'Give it up, don't you mean, darling?'

'No, not exactly.' Didn't he realise that flats as well as work were hard to find, and she had no wish to be looking for both in a few weeks time.

'But you'll be living with me!' he said patiently, 'I know it will take a bit of getting used to but it won't be forever and I'll give you all the help I can.'

It was then that she knew she couldn't do it, he was asking too much! He expected her to sacrifice everything, but promised nothing for the future. Any pleasure might soon be swallowed up in pain. For Lawton's sake, as well as her own, it would be better to call the whole thing off. Instead of the relaxed playmate he desired, he would be getting a girl increasingly prey to unhappiness and nerves. It would never work out!

'I can't do it, Lawton, I'm sorry,' she was off the sofa, rushing away from him before he could stop her.

'Neale!' he exclaimed, coming after her, looking slightly stunned. 'What's come over you, darling?' he asked when, having forgotten the door was locked and he had the key, she turned and faced him like a small cornered animal, her eyes desperate.

'I want the key!' numbly she held out a shaking hand.

'Damn the key!' he exclaimed tersely, 'I want to know what's gone wrong this time? One minute we're planning a honeymoon trip—well, not exactly. . . !'

'I don't want to hear anymore!' she interrupted wildly. 'Can't you just believe I've changed my mind!'

'No!' he snapped, angry frustration flaring in his eyes. 'You can't treat me like this, Neale, and continue to get away with it. I demand an explanation.'

She saw he was pale, a white ring round his mouth, and her lips trembled. He had straightened her dress, now she hugged her arms round herself to try and prevent him from seeing how upset she was. 'I haven't an explanation to give,' she whispered. 'At least, not one you haven't already heard. . . .'

'So that's it!' his exclamation of disgust burned her ears. 'I realise you've been seeing Tony—I suppose you've discovered you're still in love with him, and leading me on was your way of seeking revenge for what I did to you? Mistakenly I forced you along a path you would never have taken voluntarily, then I destroyed your innocence which, thanks to the besotted state I was in, I had no idea you were still keeping for him. No wonder you hate me!'

'Lawton!' she breathed aghast, 'It's not like that! And Tony's married. . . .'

'Enough!' his voice hit her with thunderous force. 'Let's have no more lies! Do you recall the last occasion I was at your flat, when your lover turned up? Well, either you told him who I was, or he recognised me, for the next morning he rang and informed me he was getting a divorce. Fool that I was, I laughed at him. I just didn't believe that after all he had put you through, you'd go back to him, but now I see how your twisted little mind works. I'd have been a much wiser man if I'd bowed out when you first rejected me.'

Horrified, Neale stared at him, trying to tell him that none of this was true and that she was shocked at what Tony had done, but just as she opened her mouth he opened the door and thrust her through it.

'Will you just shut up and go,' he snarled. 'And please bear in mind that I have no wish to see you again!'

In the hall, Neale stumbled blindly into June. 'We're just leaving,' June broke off what she was saying to her husband to shoot out a detaining hand as Neale would have rushed past her. 'Is Lawton seeing you home later, Neale, or can we drop you?'

Neale almost skidded to a stop. June was the last person she wanted to see. Futilely she tried to restore some order to her tumbled hair and to hide her hot cheeks. June must have every reason to be glancing at her curiously.

As June's expression changed to anxiety as tears began filling Neale's eyes, Neale bent her head, saying quickly, 'I'd appreciate it very much if you would.'

She didn't hear Lawton behind her. She had no idea he was there until he flung her coat roughly over her arm. 'You left it in the library,' he said harshly, ignoring her drowning eyes.

Utterly mortified, Neale stared at the carpet as he spoke to the others. 'Can we go now?' she whispered to June, 'I have a headache.'

'Nothing to what you deserve,' Lawton grated harshly, swinging on his heel.

The following morning, Neale prayed June wouldn't ring. She was aware that June was concerned for her, that she wasn't just consumed by curiosity as to what was going on, but she couldn't talk to her about what had happened between Lawton and herself yet. Perhaps one day she might find it possible to tell her something but, right now, her wounds were too raw. There had been no opportunity for June to ask anything in the taxi that had taken them home as Freddy and another couple had been there.

Rex was in a grumpy mood. 'Looks like the morning after the night before for both of you!' Mildred said tartly, after Neale had snapped at her and Rex had taken her to task over the kind of mistake he usually ignored.

Neale mumbled an apology but paid little attention. I have to leave, she kept thinking wildly. Lawton might walk in any minute. How was she going to endure the constant possibility of running into him? She would have had to leave in any case. It had been crazy to imagine she could have come back here after she had been his mistress, but if that side of the situation had resolved itself, there was still the question of her heartache. Her mind churned frantically. He thinks I was out for revenge so what's to stop him having it on me? He could make my life hell just by letting me catch a glimpse of him occasionally.

Mildred returned from lunch, humour restored, bubbling with excitement. 'Guess who I've just seen?' she exclaimed triumphantly. 'Mr Baillie and that beautiful model he's been running round with. Just before they got into his Rolls, he gave her a lovely kiss. I could almost have touched them!' she lamented, 'and I didn't have my camera!'

So that was on again! Pain gathered in Neale's throat as she managed some light remark without being aware of what she was saying. Perhaps it had never been off? Lawton had been furious with her, believing all the wrong things, but she had never gone out with anyone else, all the time she had known him.

She tried to concentrate on her work but the agony generating from the previous evening increased until she was gazing at everything blindly. She had to pull herself together! If she went on like this what use would she be to anybody? It was no good feeling bitter towards Tony for even if she could convince Lawton that Tony's phone call could only have been the result of a vindictive mind, it wouldn't alter the basic issues between Lawton and herself. It might be even better to let Lawton remain convinced that his theories were the right ones, rather than run even a faint risk of having him pursuing her again.

Neale was puzzled that after managing to do so little all day, by the time she reached home she felt worn out. When June rang almost as soon as she closed the door, she said hello with a sigh of resignation.

'I intended having a word with you, this afternoon,' June exclaimed. 'But I called to see Lawton first and was told to shut up at the first mention of your name and escorted very firmly back to my car. I was going to defy him but he looked so—— Oh, I just don't know! Well, anyway, my courage failed me and I decided to wait and give you a ring instead.'

Neale drew a deep, evasive breath. 'I can't speak for Lawton, June. I'll admit we keep having little disagreements, but there's nothing for you to worry about.'

'That's what you say!' June's voice rose dryly, 'You didn't happen to see your face last night, or Lawton's! I just didn't sleep!'

A few minutes later, Neale replaced her receiver with relief, thankful that she had been able to convince June that nothing was as bad as it might seem. Lawton, she had told June, had lunched with Nina York, and her additional hint that she was thinking of going out for dinner herself, had helped.

Pulling off her damp mac, after she had finished speaking to June, Neale hung it up absently. She could have gone out for dinner, there was always some man at the office asking her to. Perhaps it was time she began accepting their invitations? On the whole they were a nice lot and she'd give anything to have something to take her mind off Lawton.

When the phone rang for the second·time, she was tempted to ignore it until her accelerating heart suggested it might be the one person she was trying to forget. But when she rather apprehensively snatched up the receiver again, she was startled to find it was her father, ringing all the way from Australia. She had forgotten her parents usually rang around Christmas time and it was near enough.

'Is Mummy with you?' she asked, after she had enquired how they were both keeping.

'No,' Robert Curtis's voice sharpened, 'She's out. I can't talk long, Neale, this call is expensive. I just wondered if Tony has been to see you?'

'He has. . . .' she admitted cautiously.

'Well?'

'Well, what?' she asked hastily.

'For heaven's sake, girl!' Robert rushed on, as if he was actually counting the seconds, 'He wants to marry you, doesn't he?'

'He's already married,' Neale reminded him.

'He told your mother and me he's getting a divorce.'

'I don't care what he's going to get, Dad,' Neale retorted coldly, 'I'm not interested anymore.'

Her father sighed, she could hear it quite clearly. 'You might consider us, Neale.'

Consider them? Neale frowned. 'How do you mean?'

'It would be a great help if we knew you were safely married and we didn't have to worry about you anymore.'

Or even think about me! Neale thought bitterly. Aloud she said, 'I'll give you a ring in a week or so, Dad. Perhaps Mummy will be with you then?'

'Neale!'

'Listen, Dad,' she said quickly. 'I have a good job, a nice flat, good friends. You certainly don't have to worry about me. Give my love to Mum. . . .'

Hypocrite, Neale reproached herself later—yet she did love her parents in a way. The question was, did they love her? She supposed it wasn't their fault that they had never seemed to want anyone but themselves. She could understand how a daughter alone in England might be easier to forget if she had a husband to look after her but they couldn't expect her to get married for that reason alone. Her father wouldn't have believed her if she had told him she would never be married now that Lawton didn't want her, and it might be kinder to let him go on hoping.

Neale scarcely slept that night and like the previous day, couldn't concentrate when she got to the office. She thought a drive to the hotel would help clear her head and when it didn't she spent most of the afternoon wandering on the beach, giving in helplessly to an urgent desire to review her traumatic relationship with Lawton. The cries of the gulls were as desolate, on this winter's day, as the pounding of the seas, yet in some strange way the very wildness of the elements helped her. They seemed to wipe away all pride and pretence, to release in her a need to be completely honest with herself.

She had been terribly confused. Now, in the cold, crisp air, she began seeing things very differently. Lawton had asked her to go to Greece with him and she had refused because he hadn't mentioned love or marriage, yet didn't she already belong to him as though they were already married? And without his help mightn't she have remained forever in the frozen, inhibited state she had been in? He had taught her, with infinite tenderness and patience, how to be happy again, how to find pleasure in the simple things of the senses, and then, with a kindness and care she realised she wouldn't find in many men, he had made her whole again. All this she had rejected, all because he hadn't offered her a wedding ring! She had taken everything but been unwilling to give anything in return. On the

lonely beach tears began running down Neale's cheeks
as she feared that, even now, it might be too late to put
things right.

Driving back to London, she knew what she must do.
The city, with its festive lights welcomed her but she
drove through them blindly. The streets were thronged
with late afternoon shoppers and she remembered with
a pang that it was almost Christmas. She wondered
hollowly how she would be spending Christmas? She
was going to ask Lawton to forgive her but even if he
did he might not want to have anything more to do
with her.

On reaching the office, she rang his secretary straight
away to see if he would see her but Miss Hepworth said
he had just gone. Since Neale was doubtful about
arriving at his apartment without permission, she
decided to go home and try to contact him from there.
If he told her he had no wish to see her, it might be
easier to endure over the telephone than possibly having
his door slammed in her face.

It was half-past eight before she gathered sufficient
courage to dial his number and when he answered her
call she found herself unable to speak. He must have
thought it was someone having a joke for he asked
quite sharply who was there?

'Neale,' she breathed.

'Yes?' he barked, when she said no more.

His acid tone didn't help but she forced herself to
continue regardless. 'I—I'd like to see you for a few
minutes, Lawton. If it's convenient, that is?'

Another pause, then slowly. 'Neale, will there be any
point in this? I've had a long day and was counting on
an early night, or a peaceful one, anyway. However, if
you feel it's important. . . .?'

'It is!' she cried feverishly.

'Very well,' he agreed reluctantly. 'Come when you
like: I'll be in all evening.'

Twenty minutes later she was pressing the bell of his

apartment. Would Nina be there with him? The question haunted Neale as she waited for Lawton to answer the door. When he did she suddenly realised she had nothing adequately prepared to say to him.

As he looked at her, the lack of expression on his hard, handsome face gave no clue to his feelings, but a certain hardness in his eyes and mouth wasn't encouraging. He was wearing a pair of dark trousers with a crew-necked jersey which, for a heart-stopping moment, took her back to the Caribbean.

'Are you coming in?' he asked politely, 'Or do you intend explaining what you've come about, out here?'

She stumbled quickly past him, flushing as she realised she was staring. 'I'd rather come inside, that is if I'm not interrupting anything?'

Behind her, Lawton closed the door with a decisive snap. 'If by that you mean, do I have company, then the answer is no. I told you, I'm tired.'

Neale shivered at the coldness of his voice as he almost pushed her into the lounge. Nervously she unzipped the anorak she had flung on hastily over a pair of jeans. Feeling his disparaging glance on her masses of wind-tossed hair, she regretted not taking more care over her appearance. She must look like a scarecrow and he probably couldn't wait to get rid of her. It was a relief that Miss York wasn't here but that didn't mean she wouldn't be, later!

That Lawton made no attempt to relieve her of her coat only increased her suspicions. He obviously had no intention of touching her if he could help it. He didn't even ask her to sit down, he merely stood, dark brows slightly lifted, waiting, without apparent interest, to hear the reason for her visit.

With an unconsciously nervous gesture, Neale brushed a trembling hand over her hair. 'I wanted you to know that you were wrong about Tony,' she began haltingly, 'He means nothing to me and I haven't been seeing him.'

'So . . .?'

He wasn't making it easy. She looked at him, her face pale, her eyes reflecting her inner agony. 'You don't say whether you believe me?'

He shrugged, watching her enigmatically. 'Is it important whether I do or not?'

'If you don't,' she replied desperately, 'then there's not much point in going on. Even if Tony hadn't been married it would have made no difference, I just don't feel anything for him anymore. For some reason his marriage is going through a sticky phase and when he's in London he's looking for something to take his mind off his troubles. I don't believe he loves me anymore than I love him.'

'Then why did he ring me?'

'I honestly don't know,' she confessed. 'I only remember that when we were younger he couldn't stand being thwarted in any way. That evening he called at my flat, when you were there, I hadn't asked him to call, despite what he said, and I'm afraid I wasn't very nice to him afterwards. I can't prove any of this, of course.'

'You don't have to,' Lawton said flatly. 'I think I realised a long time ago, Neale, that you didn't love him anymore, but when a man is jealous and insecure in his relations with a woman, Neale, and this time I'm talking of myself, he isn't too fussy over his choice of weapons. However,' he held up a hand, stepping back as she stepped forward, 'this doesn't change the main issue between us. You may not care for Tony anymore but he left you with a total inability to face the future with any kind of confidence. And that is what I can't fight.'

Neale stiffened against another involuntary attempt to get near him. In some ways Lawton was right, but, in others so wrong! If he had loved her she could have shown him weeks ago just how completely he had cured her of any hang-ups.

She looked at him, swallowing hard. 'I came, tonight, Lawton, to tell you I'm not frightened of the future. If you still want me, I'll come to Greece with you, or do whatever you wish.'

'You'll come to Greece?' Fury glittered suddenly in the blue eyes. It was he, this time, who closed the gap between them to allow his hands to descend like a vice on her shoulders. 'Is this some fresh whim, Neale? What happens when I want to make love to you? How long will it take you to change your mind again?'

'I wouldn't.'

'Let's see?' Roughly he jerked her into his arms, crushing her to him as his mouth ground relentlessly down on hers. Neale whimpered at the pain and sensation of electricity vibrating through them, jolting her system until she could have cried out in alarm. She hadn't wanted to remember the waves of violent emotion which could render her almost senseless when Lawton kissed her but tonight he seemed determined to remind her of the fires which always threatened to burn them up. With a low moan, she went limp, then as she suddenly feared she might completely lose control, she began struggling against him.

'Please!' she whispered, her lips throbbing, her body shaking.

'You see,' pushing her away, his eyes scorched her with contempt, 'even a kiss is enough to make you have second thoughts. So, no thanks. I just haven't the stomach for any more. I'll go to Greece alone.'

She turned from him blindly, her voice hoarse. 'I shouldn't have come.'

He caught her, swinging her back to him savagely, 'Why did you come, Neale? This time I want the truth!'

She could see he wasn't going to leave her an ounce of pride. He didn't know any she'd had left was already gone. 'I love you, Lawton,' she couldn't look at him as she confessed it but she imagined the state she was in would convince him. 'I realised when you asked me to

be your mistress that you would only be embarrassed if
I told you. . . .'

'Neale!' he broke in explosively. 'You might drop one
bombshell on a man and get away with it but never
two. I'm not convinced that you love me but I do know
I never asked you to be my mistress.'

'But you sent me a key to this apartment,' her eyes
flew to his in bewilderment. 'You said you had told the
commissionaire I'd be moving in, and the other night,
when you asked me to go to Greece with you, nothing
you said even hinted at a permanent relationship.
That's why I was reluctant to give up my flat or my job.
I felt I had to have something to come back to after you
tired of me. Because I loved you I really thought I could
be your mistress—it was when you actually mentioned
that it wouldn't be forever that I suddenly knew I
couldn't do it.'

'Neale!' with a smothered gròan and looking
completely astounded and angry, Lawton almost
roughly caught her in his arms, interrupting her broken
sentences grimly. 'You've got it all wrong, my darling!
It was never my intention to ask you to be my mistress.
I want you for my wife! I've had a special licence in my
desk ever since we returned from St Lucia. The night of
the party, I was going to show it to you when you went
all cold and furious on me. Didn't you realise . . .? Had
you no idea?'

'How could I?' she whispered, her face as tortured as
his, 'I told you I loved you in the Caribbean but you
didn't even reply, and you seemed almost glad to be
leaving.'

'I was,' he groaned, 'but not for the reasons you seem
to think.' Threading his fingers through her hair, he
tilted her head, making her look at him. 'I wanted you
the first time I saw you and it nearly killed me that after
waiting so long for something I had thought would
never happen, I discovered I'd fallen in love with a girl
who didn't love me. You were so full of inhibitions

which I didn't understand until you told me about Tony. Even then I didn't get it right. I believed you'd had an affair with him and realising I had been wrong about that didn't help.'

He sighed and gently kissed her mouth before he went on. 'After the first time we made love, I was going to ask you to marry me but I feared, if I did, you might believe I'd felt forced to because of what had happened. And, because of all you had suffered with Tony, I daren't rush you. I thought it might be wiser to give you a breathing space to get used to the idea of belonging to me. What I didn't allow for was the strength of my own feelings. After only two days I found it impossible to keep my hands off you, which was why I was relieved when the call came from London. Away from the romantic atmosphere of the Caribbean I hoped we could work something out, but instead things appeared to go from bad to worse. Before I went to the continent, I sent you the key to my apartment, so you could be there when I returned, when I was determined to make you agree to marry me. I told John, the commissionaire, whom I've known for years, incidentally, that you'd be coming so he would let you past. And, yes, I did say you'd be moving in, but he knew I didn't mean as my mistress. I distinctly recall him saying, 'It happens to us all in the end, Mr Baillie.'

Neale tried to smile but remembered her pain. 'If only I had known.'

Lawton's mouth twisted ironically. 'I wrote that note in a terrible hurry but I never dreamt you would take it the wrong way.'

Afterwards, it struck Neale as odd that at this juncture she should find herself asking what, considering everything else, must have been an irrelevant question. 'What does the M stand for?'

'Marcus,' he confessed humbly, 'I hope you don't mind?'

This time she managed to smile but the light swiftly

died from her eyes. 'You don't know what that note did to me,' she said reproachfully. 'You see I had no idea you wanted to marry me, and even when I agreed to go to Greece with you, you said we would come back here but it wouldn't be forever.'

His frowned deepened as he muttered tersely. 'I seem to have made a hash of just about everything, haven't I? What I meant, darling, was that we'd probably be living in the West Indies. That's what I had in mind for the island I bought there. Or if you didn't like the idea of living abroad, I was planning a home in the country— for our children. I have to keep the apartment, of course, for when I'm here on business, but it's never been home to me.'

'Oh, darling, I've been such a fool!' Neale put her arms round his neck and hugged him tightly.

'We both have, I think,' his eyes glowed into hers, 'I've been through hell, I was so mad with jealousy.'

'Without reason. Not like me,' she added, looking at him darkly. 'Whenever I saw you with Miss York I wanted to scratch her eyes out.'

'Did you really?' he laughed softly, as if the thought of Neale being jealous delighted him. 'I'm not sure if I should tell you, my love, but the only time I've been with Nina was in a crowd. The worst I was ever guilty of was kissing her in front of your secretary, hoping wickedly, I confess, that she would go straight to you.'

'She did!' Neale retorted with feeling.

'I didn't ask her to the party I gave, you know,' he said ruefully. 'Like your Tony she is good at fabrication. That kiss your secretary saw was the nearest I've been to another woman since the moment I laid eyes on you.'

'Oh, Lawton,' with stars in her eyes, Neale breathed, 'I do love you!'

'And I you,' he laughed triumphantly. 'We will be married tomorrow and spend Christmas in Greece. Unless you'd rather visit your parents?'

'No.' She would try and explain about her parents, one day. She might even tell him about her father's phone call about Tony, but she didn't feel it was something that couldn't wait. Not like the sudden clamour inside her to belong to Lawton completely, in every way. 'I'd rather go to Greece,' she said shyly, her cheeks pink.

'Afterwards,' he kissed her tenderly, 'we'll have a real honeymoon in the Caribbean, whether we decide to live there or not.'

Neale trembled through the ecstasy enveloping her, 'I can't believe this is really happening.'

Lawton went very still, his eyes intent on her glowing young beauty. 'You could give me a chance to convince you,' he suggested huskily. 'But I warn you it might take all night.'

She pretended to consider while, in reality, her heart was singing. A lifetime stretched before her and something told her it wouldn't be long enough for either of them, so it seemed sensible to add every hour they could find. And, loving each other so deeply, whatever they did couldn't be wrong. Lawton said he had loved her from the beginning and it had been this way for her, too. This was why, she realised, she had been able to give herself to him so willingly on the yacht. It had been a commitment for as long as she lived, and beyond, and, as such would never be something to regret.

When she smiled at him, her face was so radiant that Lawton didn't waste time on any more words. He simply picked her up and carried her through to his bedroom, kissing her lips on the way and still keeping his mouth on hers as he laid her gently on the bed and began making love to her. Soon they were both naked and whispering passionately of the love reflected in their eyes. Every barrier seemed to be removed as he gathered her possessively to him, the hunger in him becoming more apparent with every moment that passed.

'I've been deprived for so long,' he growled. 'You can't expect me to be easily satisfied.'

'I hope not,' she murmured cheekily, and was punished with a sharp nip on her bare thigh. Then, as she winced but flung her arms tightly round him, the world faded and only their love and mounting passion remained a total reality.

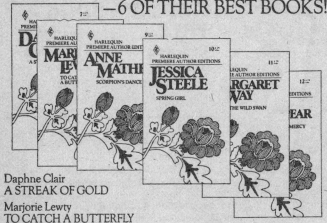